THE BLINGSTERS

OLD SCHOOL MYSTERIES
BOOK 1

ANDREA C. NEIL

For my grandma, Delphine L. Neil.
Thanks for letting me tell you all those stories.

CHAPTER 1

Griffin pulled her rental car in behind her grandma's Mercedes and killed the engine. The flight from Dallas to Miami International had been crowded and cramped. These days, air travel seemed to be a form of purgatory inflicted on people whose only crime was wanting to get somewhere faster than if they drove. At least the payoff for some travelers was a vacation. But not for Griffin.

Even though she'd been running the AC full blast since she left the airport, she could still smell the sea through the rental car's vents. It made sense, since the ocean was so close that she could get out of the car, walk ten steps, and be on the beach. Which is exactly what she did.

She stood where the end of the sidewalk met the sand and looked out at the water. It had been a long time since she'd been to a coast. Ten years, maybe? There weren't very many beaches in Fort Worth, Texas where they lived. Her husband Brian kept promising they would take a Hawaiian vacation "sometime soon," but he'd been saying that since they got married five years earlier.

Yep, there was nothing like the beach. But unfortunately, she wasn't there to relax on the sand. She inhaled the salty ocean air and turned back to the house and the sleek, silver AMG E 53. She was a touch jealous of her grandma's sweet ride. They'd all heard about it of course, and it was one of the reasons she was now in the Florida Keys on this sticky September day.

Marge Flanders was Griffin's grandma on her dad's side, and Griffin called her G-ma. Three months earlier G-ma had left out of Miami on a senior's cruise to the Bahamas. She'd gotten back to Florida okay, but never managed to make it home to Enid, Oklahoma, where she lived in an apartment complex down the street from Griffin's parents' house.

G-ma called home once a week and always told Griffin's dad that she was fine and loving her new friends and fast-paced life. But honestly, how fast-paced could your life be when you were in your seventies?

She explained that she needed a change. This was news to the family, because everyone thought she had been happy with her life in Enid. There was the senior center of course, and mall walking, and playing cards with a few old pals. Sounded pretty nice to Griffin.

Griffin's dad Riff, the older of G-ma's two sons, said she would be fine in Florida and that they shouldn't worry. He said G-ma was a grownup and could sow her big-city oats if she wanted to. He was convinced that she'd come home eventually, like when she ran out of money or got tired of living by the ocean. Whichever happened to come first.

However, when word got back to the family that G-ma had up and bought herself a German-made car, that had been the last straw. Griffin's parents sent her out to the coast to put an end to G-ma's madness and bring her back home. Her bridge club was suffering without her, after all. And it wasn't like Griffin was doing anything else anyway—she'd just been laid off from her job as a financial analyst for a government agency that she was told not to mention by name. They'd let her go after eight years of service without an explanation, the lousy jerks. She hadn't found a new job yet, so she agreed to be her grandmother's bounty hunter.

Now here she was, in North Key Largo, outside the beach house Marge rented with three other retirees. It had taken a bit of finagling for Griffin to find exactly where her grandma was staying, but suffice it to say she still had a few favors she could call in from friends at her old job.

She looked up at the house, which sat on stilts, creating a carport underneath. It was the weirdest setup she'd ever seen. No basement? Where did everyone go when a tornado came through? It wasn't natural. And how did these fragile retirees navigate those steep stairs?

She shrugged off her questions and steeled her resolve. No sense in putting it off any longer. She climbed the wooden staircase to the front door, knocked, and waited.

Nothing.

There were two other cars in the carport in addition to the Mercedes—a greyish-blue 2020 Lexus convertible and a black 2018 BMW X3—so Griffin assumed at least one other person was around to answer the door. It was already 10:00 a.m. Didn't seniors get up at impossibly early hours? Another question she added to her growing list. She knocked again.

Still nothing.

After a few seconds more she tried turning the doorknob, and wouldn't you know it, it was unlocked. She took that as a standing invitation to enter and walked right in, pausing in the foyer. The scene that confronted Griffin surprised the living daylights out of her.

The place was an absolute mess. No way on earth could this be where her grandma lived! Her G-ma was one of the tidiest people Griffin knew. Nothing was ever out of place at her apartment, let alone dusty. But this house looked worse than Griffin's second cousin Harold's apartment, and he had the forgivable excuse of being "one of god's special children," according to G-ma.

The decor seemed questionable, and that was putting it

politely. The pile of the baby-blue shag carpet was so high that Griffin left a wake behind her as she walked into the living room. The wallpaper was also blue, a few shades darker than the carpet, with a subtle scallop-shell pattern in flocked velvet. Couches that looked like floral-upholstered freight trains sat at right angles to each other, and a coffee table resembling a giant glass ashtray completed the tableau. A television the size of Griffin's Subaru hung on the wall opposite one of the couches, and under it sat an entertainment unit with three or four different gaming consoles spewing cables and remotes onto the floor.

Red plastic cups littered the carpet, along with bits of popcorn, a few cigarette butts, and little pellets that appeared to be raisins, though Griffin couldn't be sure, and she had no interest in investigating them further. Natural Light beer cans lay scattered everywhere—on the coffee table, the floor, and stacked in a pyramid within a collection of Hummel figurines in a tall, narrow bookshelf. In a display of debauchery worthy of a frat party, the half-wall separating the living room from the kitchen was home to approximately forty empty liquor bottles.

Griffin's jaw dropped. All she could think about was how she would explain to her dad that his mother was living like a college girl gone wild. He wasn't going to take the news very well.

She felt like she was trekking through mud as she walked farther into the house—she would take a step and then sink. Lord only knew what might be in that jungle of shag carpet, lost to all but the most powerful of vacuum cleaners. As if on cue, her right shoe landed on something much harder than carpet. It felt big, like a golf ball, but she couldn't see anything. She moved her foot out of the way, kneeled to examine the imprint in the carpet, and pulled out a diamond so clear and sparkly and brilliant that it really did seem as big as a golf ball. She had no words to describe her surprise and confusion, so she just let out a small gasp.

It was official: things had gotten weird. Griffin stood up and scratched the back of her head with one hand while gripping the rock tightly with the other. It was then that she noticed a figure sprawled on a chaise longue out on the balcony right off the living room. Oh dear, she thought, a diamond *and* a dead body? She crept closer to the open sliding glass door and heard snoring so loud it competed with the sound of the waves pounding on the beach a mere two hundred yards away.

The man lay passed out on his back, one hand on his round belly, the other hanging off the side of the chair. He looked to be around the same age as her grandma, and Griffin hoped with all her might that it wasn't her G-ma's boyfriend, because something about him seemed more than a little unsavory.

A seagull landed on the balcony railing and eyed the man's stomach, encased in a pink polo golf shirt that lay untucked over brown leisure pants. The bird looked almost gleeful. It seemed like a good time for Griffin to walk away.

"I'll let you have your privacy," she whispered to the bird.

She needed to find her G-ma. Stat.

CHAPTER 2

When she turned away from the balcony, Griffin ran into something that hadn't been behind her a moment earlier. It was a very small woman, and the top of her wispy white hair only came up to Griffin's collar bones. Griffin gripped the diamond tightly in her hand and hoped the woman hadn't noticed it.

"Hi," she said to the woman's hair, slipping the gem into the pocket of her chinos.

"Hello young lady," the woman said to Griffin's boobs. She peered up at Griffin's face and her bright blue eyes twinkled. But something besides mirth lay right beneath the surface, and Griffin couldn't figure out what it was. "You must be Marge's daughter," the lady continued.

Griffin did a mental face palm. Being called her grandmother's daughter was something she wished would happen less often. She wasn't sure if it was because her G-ma looked so youthful, or if Griffin happened to look a lot older than her age, which was only thirty-two.

"I'm her granddaughter. Griffin Beckett." She stuck out her hand to shake, but the woman just sized her up, giving her a full once-over before pulling her bathrobe tighter around her slight frame. Which had been a good move because Griffin was about to get an eyeful of something she had no desire to see.

"Well," said the woman. "That's nice."

So much for introductions. Griffin shrugged and looked past her toward a hallway leading farther into the house. "Can you tell me where she is?"

"No," said the white-haired lady. She scrutinized Griffin one more time and meandered toward the kitchen.

Griffin wondered what she should do next, and silently prayed that she wouldn't find her grandma in the den of depravity she'd stumbled into. However, it was even more frightening to think of where G-ma might be if she *weren't* in the house somewhere. Was she being held there against her will? Griffin started to feel anxious and the giant gem in her pocket wasn't helping.

On her next in-breath she started coughing and couldn't seem to stop. Hopefully she wasn't allergic to large, loose diamonds. She needed a glass of water to calm her throat, so she headed for the kitchen. The tiny white-haired lady had disappeared by then, leaving Griffin alone in what could only be described as a crime scene.

Every available inch of counter space was piled high with dirty dishes and more beer cans, and the sink overflowed with food-encrusted dishes and glasses with rings of dried liquid inside. In one corner of the small space sat the largest collection of used empty pizza boxes she'd ever seen. They weren't all from the same pizza place, either.

Griffin's coughing continued and she looked around the mess with more urgency, finally finding a clean-enough glass in a cabinet and a Brita pitcher in the fridge. As she drank a half glass of water, she noticed the stove was spotless. Two clean pots rested on the back burners, and the whole thing was free of trash and dust and dirt. Most curious.

Her throat was feeling better now, and Griffin set her glass on a stack of plastic bowls in the sink. She contemplated washing her item, but what would be the point? It would have been the polite thing to do, but under the circumstances, it was doubtful anyone would notice.

Griffin marched down the hall. The first door she came to on her right was closed but unlocked, so she flung it wide only to find ... Well, let's just say two people were in there, and she had been raised up too politely to put into words what they were doing to each other. As luck would have it, neither of the people participating in the questionable acrobatics were her grandma.

"Sorry!" she barked as she squeezed her eyes shut and raised her forearm to her face, for good measure.

No one said anything back to her. All Griffin could hear was the squeaking of bedsprings, so she pulled the door shut. It took a minute before she was ready to open her eyes though, and she wasn't sure she would ever get the image out of her head.

The next door opened into a bathroom. Empty, praise be.

At the end of the hall was another closed door, and Griffin opened it, but with more caution this time. On the bed, which was still made, lay a woman splayed face-down on a quilted floral duvet cover that looked straight out of the 1970s. She wore a cocktail dress, her high heels were still strapped her feet, and she snored like a passed-out trucker. The woman was quite small, perhaps even tinier than the white-haired lady who had snuck up on her in the living room. Griffin's G-ma was, by Griffin's recollection, about the same height as herself, so this woman probably wasn't her. The tiny lady sported a bob of jet-black hair. Her grandmother was more of a purple-tint kind of gal, but maybe she had changed more than her address recently. Griffin crept up to the bed to take a peek at the woman.

The woman's face wasn't visible, being nestled in the duvet cover, but once Griffin had gotten within a foot of the bed the sleeping figure emitted a surprisingly loud snarfling noise, lifted her head, and moaned, "Buuuuutter." Then another face-plant. Griffin backed away as stealthily as she could and left the room. Not G-ma.

Only two more rooms remained, and Griffin made her way back down the hallway to the next door. It was open a crack, maybe two inches at most, so she peeked in. And there she was, her sweet G-ma, lying asleep in her bed on her back. Alone.

"G-ma!" cried Griffin, so happy to have found her. She ran to the bed and jumped onto it, bouncing into place right beside her still-sleeping grandma.

Marge awoke with a start and a loud yell and began pummeling Griffin. "Floyd! Watch out for the hamsters!" she said as she kept hitting her granddaughter.

"Grandma, it's me, Griffin!" Griffin tried to shield her face, but not before her grandma caught her square on the temple. "Ow!"

The pummeling stopped. "Oh," said Marge. "Griffin? Goodness gracious! What are you doing here?"

Griffin unfurled herself from her defensive position as Marge reached over to her nightstand and chose one of two pairs of glasses resting by a cup of water that thankfully didn't have a set of dentures floating in it, like you'd expect in a movie or cartoon. Marge put on her glasses and gave Griffin a good look. She craned her neck to peer closer.

"Dear, you really should do something about those enormous pores," she said.

Griffin looked her grandma in the eyes—each of which looked as big and round as dinner plates behind the thick lenses of her glasses. It was disturbing, in an insect-like way. "G-ma, you—"

Marge's arm darted out and she put her hand over Griffin's mouth. "Could you please stop yelling? Grandma had a little too much Natty Light with dinner."

Griffin's brow furrowed. She hadn't been yelling. Her grandma never used to drink, except on Sundays, when she would have "one beer for Jesus." But this was Saturday and Griffin was pretty sure that Jesus had better taste in beer than Natural Light.

"You've got your super magnifier lenses on," Griffin whispered.

G-ma took off her glasses and squinted at them. "Well for the love of Pete, would you look at that!" She exchanged her eyewear for the other pair of glasses on the nightstand. "Oh yes, much better. My dear Griffin! You're a sight for sore eyes." She wrapped her granddaughter in a snuggly grandma hug, but after a few seconds shoved her away. "I'll ask you again. What on earth are you doing here?"

"I've come to get you and take you back home."

"Ha! Good one. I'm not going anywhere." She crossed her arms in front of her chest.

"Dad's worried about you. We all are. What is this place?" Griffin flicked her thumb toward the door. "Who are these people? Are you in a sorority or something?"

G-ma propped herself up so that her back leaned against the headboard, and Griffin did the same. "Kind of."

"Right. Could you get any more cryptic?"

"Yes," Marge answered. "Yes I could."

They were silent for a moment, and Griffin thought about telling her G-ma about the diamond in her pocket but then decided against it. She listened to the sound of the waves coming through the open bedroom window. That part was nice, at least.

"G-ma, who's Floyd?" Griffin asked.

"Huh?"

"And what was that about the hamsters?"

"Griffy, stop talking nonsense."

"Okay, fine. Then can we talk about what's going on here?"

"Can I at least go to the bathroom first?"

"Tell you what. How about we get out of here and I take you to lunch someplace?" Maybe if she could get her grandma to neutral territory, she'd have a better chance of convincing her to get on that evening's flight to DFW.

Marge's face lit up and she clapped her hands. "That sounds marvelous! Just give me a few minutes to get dressed and put on my face."

"Okay. I think I'll wait for you in the car." Griffin got up and made for the bedroom door. "While you're at it, maybe pack an overnight bag," she suggested. They could always have the rest of her grandma's things shipped home later.

"You're so cute, Griffy," said Marge, and Griffin gave her a blank stare. "You think I was born yesterday? No dice. We're doing lunch and that's it."

Griffin lowered her head. It had been worth a try. "Fine."

Marge started to get out of bed, and she let out a hearty laugh as she flipped the covers back.

"What's so funny?" asked Griffin.

"You're lucky I remembered to put my jammies on last night."

Griffin felt very lucky indeed.

"You go on down, and I'll be there directly, okay?"

"Sure thing, G-ma," said Griffin. "Hey, there's a guy sleeping on a chaise longue on your balcony. I'm not sure if he's okay or not."

"Oh," said Marge as she riffled through her closet. "That's Big Moe. He stays over sometimes if the party really gets hoppin'. He's harmless."

"He's not your boyfriend, is he?"

Marge laughed again. "Oh heck no, he's a podiatrist! Trust me, I got better taste in men than that!"

"Sure," Griffin said, and left the room. She didn't want to hear too much about her grandma's love life.

She waded through the living room again, heading toward the front door. This time through, the decor started to make her seasick.

"Hey kid!" A man's voice that sounded like gravel being pulverized in a Ninja blender called out, right before she got to the door.

Griffin froze, wondering if the man had been speaking to her. She looked back, and there stood Big Moe next to the ashtray coffee table. He seemed to be swaying more than standing. A large splotch of bird poop now adorned the hem of his shirt. Seagull 1, Old Guy 0.

His face was stern as he pointed to the shag carpet. This was it; Griffin was sure. He knew what she had taken! Why had she done it? She didn't have an answer other than she had been mesmerized by the beautiful diamond. Her hand went to her pants pocket, and she prepared for the worst.

"Have you by any chance seen my shoes?" he asked in a thick New York accent.

Griffin now looked to where he'd been pointing: his bare feet. She glanced around the room, but no men's shoes were in sight. They could have been lost somewhere in the pile of the carpet, gone forever, but that was not her problem.

She opened her mouth, but no words came out. All she could manage was to shake her head and head out the door.

CHAPTER 3

Once she was sure Griffin had left the house, Marge made her way across the hall to get ready in the bathroom. Vern had the master bedroom and her own bathroom, but Marge had to share with her other two roommates. It wasn't too bad—they seemed to take better care of that shared space than they did the kitchen. The only downside was that she had more ground to cover when she needed to use the facilities, which happened multiple times a night if she had too much beer before bed.

She washed her face and properly re-mussed her hair. She only put on a minimal amount of makeup—a little bit of lipstick went a long way in making her feel presentable. Back home in Oklahoma, she didn't have to worry about things like that very much. Sure, the Enid Senior Center got going on Saturday nights, but it was usually (and literally) the same old crowd every week, month, and year. She couldn't remember now what had possessed her to go on a senior's cruise in the first place; she never did things like that. But she sure was glad she'd done it. Now that she'd met the Blingsters, she realized that over the years she had forgotten how much fun life could be.

When she felt suitably refreshed, Marge went back to her bedroom and changed into one of her favorite jumpsuits. She found a matching purse, put on some sandals, and left, closing the door behind her. She'd been thinking about getting a lock, but all the roommates did a good job of respecting one of the most important house rules, which was to stay the heck out of other people's bedrooms.

"Good morning," said Vern as Marge came into the living room. "Can we talk to you for a minute?"

Vern sat on one of the big blue couches, and Big Moe and Smitty were seated on the other. Each of them held a mug of steaming coffee. Marge was surprised they'd been able to find the coffee maker; when she had tried the day before she'd been unable to locate it.

"My granddaughter is waiting for me," said Marge, hoping for a reprieve from whatever they were about to throw at her. It was too early in the day, and she was too hung over to deal with Vern and Big Moe.

"It will only take one minute," said Big Moe.

Vern pulled her bathrobe tightly across her chest. It was a good move, Marge thought. They'd all noticed that Big Moe had a wandering eye, and in a house full of so much senior hotness, they had to be vigilant. Big Moe was married, and his wife was more than a little bit scary. They'd never known him to stray, but he seemed to do a lot of looking.

"Say, what's that on your shirt?" asked Marge, pointing to his protruding belly.

"What?" he said and looked down at his stomach. He found the hem of his pink polo shirt with his fingers and pulled the fabric away from his midsection to get a better view. "That looks like bird crap," he said, sounding perplexed.

Smitty's black bob swung with a *whoosh* as she turned her head to investigate Big Moe's shirt. Her face scrunched up with disapproval and she scooted farther away from him on the couch.

Marge was also perplexed about the bird crap, but she was not in the mood to bother getting to the bottom of that particular mystery.

Big Moe held the hem of the fabric away from his body as he looked around for something to clean his shirt with, but the only things within reach that would have been suitable were dirtier than what he had on.

As Big Moe fiddled with his crappy shirt, Marge surveyed the room, disheartened that no one had cleaned anything up from their rager the night before. It felt like they always left the mess for her to clean up, which she had done the first couple of times, but no more. That was not in her job description as a Blingster, even if she was the newest member. "Whaddya say we get us a cleaning lady to come in and take care of all this mess?" she asked.

Vern looked like she was considering the idea but stayed silent.

Big Moe said, "Do you think that is wise, under the circumstances?"

"First of all," said Marge, putting one hand on her hip, "you don't live here, so you be quiet. Second, this place is a pigsty! And C, all it takes to stay out of trouble is a little attention to detail. Now surely we're smart enough to do that so we can get a cleaning lady."

"Ooh, we're getting a cleaning lady?" Big El had wandered into the living room. Marge let herself indulge in a tiny eye roll. Big El was great fun, but always had an opinion on EV-ER-Y-THING and Marge could tell she was about to weigh in with her two cents. "How's about we get us a cleaning *man*?" she suggested in her thick Scottish accent. "Like a pool boy but for kitchens."

Vern nodded. "I like where this is going."

Marge was intrigued. "Well now, that is a pretty good idea," she said.

"Don't sound too surprised, Marge, I'm known to have them from time to time."

"Fine with me, whatever," said Marge, getting frustrated now.

Griffin would be even more suspicious if she had to wait much longer.

"Right!" said Big El. She got out her phone. "Siri, find hot cleaning guys," she yelled at the screen as she walked toward the kitchen.

"One moment while I search for hot clingy gays," said her phone.

Marge knew that *hot cleaning guys* was already a dangerous search phrase, but the one Siri had come up with after not understanding Big El's accent would be far worse. Regardless, she didn't have time for such nonsense. "Now Vern, what did you want to talk to me about?" she asked.

"Big Moe here is asking about Griffin," said Vern.

"She's too young for you," Marge snapped at him, but then placed her hand over her mouth. Her eyes darted to Vern, who stifled a laugh. "I mean, what about Griffy?"

"Were you expecting her to visit?" he said in his raspy voice.

"No," said Marge. "I think my son sent her out here to check on me. He's such a sweetheart, my Riffy!"

"Riffy and Griffy?" asked Big Moe.

"Yup, and my ex was Ziffy!"

Vern closed her eyes and rubbed her forehead, appearing to be pained by something.

"What," said Marge. "You people don't use nicknames? How about 'Big Moe'?"

"I have a large family," he said. "We need nicknames to avoid confusion. We do not make them rhyme however."

"Oh well, your loss," said Marge. She looked at her watch. "Anything else?"

"You are not going to tell her anything of importance, are you?" Big Moe asked.

"Pffft! Of course not!" Marge waved a hand in the air to dismiss such a silly idea. "What happens in the Blingsters stays in the Blingsters. I know the credo!"

Big Moe nodded.

"She seems like a nice girl," said Vern.

"Oh my, yes, she is! And so smart too! So sad the FBI let her go."

"The F-B-what?" said Moe, sitting up straighter. For a second, he abandoned the hem of his shirt until the cold, wet spot touched his belly, and he caught hold of the fabric again.

"I told you about that, Vern," said Marge. "I bragged about her just the other day."

"You did," said Vern, who turned to Big Moe. "She did. It's fine. Marge is a great friend, a wonderful roommate, and a perfect canasta player. If she says her granddaughter is fine, then I believe her."

This seemed to placate Big Moe, who nodded again and relaxed. "Okay," he said.

"Alrighty then," said Marge. "I'm off to lunch with Griffy, so see ya later!"

Vern waved and Big Moe grunted, having resumed his search for something to clean his shirt with.

Marge high-stepped through the carpet to the front door. As she got out into the fresh air and descended the stairs to Griffin's waiting rental car, she started to feel better. Yes, fresh air and a good lunch would take care of everything. She loved her new friends and fun life. She felt optimistic that she could keep having fun, stay in Big Moe's good graces, and maybe spend a little time with Griffin before sending her granddaughter back to Texas. Alone.

CHAPTER 4

Marge gave directions as Griffin drove and fifteen minutes later, they were sitting in a cozy diner called Little Moe's. The view of the water from their window booth was beautiful. The diner overlooked a small bay which featured a marina on one end and a private beach on the other. In the center was a pier, complete with fishermen dotting its length. Griffin started to think she should give up on Fort Worth and that perhaps her grandmother was onto something with this Florida thing.

"Isn't it great here?" Marge put down her menu and gave Griffin a huge smile from across the booth.

"If by 'here' you mean Key Largo and by 'great' you mean this view, then yes, it's great. If you mean this restaurant, I'm not so sure." Griffin tried to put the menu down, but it stuck to her fingers for a second before landing on the tabletop with a greasy *thwap*. She hoped the sticky residue was something benign, like syrup. A whiny, rattling sound came from the hallway leading to the kitchen. It must have been a refrigeration unit of some kind, maybe an ice machine on its last legs, Griffin reckoned. The noise grated on her nerves, and she considered going back there and putting the thing out of its misery for good.

There also weren't many customers in the place—just one

woman with her young son, to be exact. An empty restaurant around lunchtime didn't bode well for the upcoming dining experience, Griffin feared.

"Little Moe's isn't much to look at, but they've got great food, you'll see. It's not very busy right now on account of there's a big fishing tournament over at the Mackerel Club. Everyone's probably having lunch there." G-ma swung her head toward the sea and her dangly earrings swooshed along for the ride. They glinted in the sunlight and caught Griffin's attention. Small diamonds dotted the length of the gold pendants. Understated yet very swanky, especially for lunch at a diner.

Griffin didn't remember her grandma looking so put together before. Then again, maybe there weren't many occasions to wear fancy earrings in Enid. Upon closer inspection, Griffin realized that Marge wore a matching diamond pendant necklace nestled in her décolletage. For a moment, she wondered if the jewelry was fake. If so, it was a high-quality fake. But no, it looked real. How could she have afforded it? Griffin knew her grandma didn't have that kind of cheddar lying around.

Marge's hair, which usually had a bluish tint, was now snow white and cut shorter than she used to wear it. It sprung out at different angles, mussed into place with styling product. Tucked into her hair on the top of her head was a pair of classic Ray-Bans. She wore a red-and-white floral jumpsuit which looked surprisingly hip, and her nails sported a fresh coat of matching red polish. Even her lipstick and purse matched. She smiled at Griffin, who felt like a bridge troll in comparison. The woman was downright glamorous.

Griffin looked down at her own outfit: chinos, flats, and a T-shirt. She wasn't going to be winning any fashion awards anytime soon. Her dark-brown hair was pulled back into a ponytail. She had to wear it that way, otherwise in the high Florida humidity, she'd look like a puff ball with eyes.

A server brought two glasses of iced tea to the table, set them down, and took out a notepad. She looked to be about G-ma's age and seemed pleasant enough, but the Dolly Parton-style wig was a little over the top for food service. Griffin hoped it was a wig, anyway.

"What'll you have?" the woman asked.

"Hi Alice! I will have the ham and cheese skillet and Griffy will have the bleu-cheese burger with extra onion rings instead of a salad." G-ma interlaced her fingers and placed her hands on the tabletop, looking up at the waitress with an air of excited expectancy.

"Sure thing, Marge," said Alice, and she walked off toward the kitchen.

"But I was going to get the kelp smoothie," said Griffin, irked that Marge had ordered for her like she was still a little kid.

G-ma frowned. "Oh Griffy, you don't come to a greasy spoon like this and get a kelp smoothie. That's a rookie move." She winked at her granddaughter but must have been able to tell Griffin was confused, because she continued with an explanation. "Just 'cause it's on the menu doesn't mean you should order it. Besides, you look a little thin. We need to fatten you up!" She stood up from her bench seat enough to lean over and pinch Griffin's cheek.

As Marge sat back down, Griffin felt another pair of eyes on her and looked to the front of the restaurant in time to see a man who stood right by the door turn away from them and stifle a laugh. Great, so much for adulting, she thought.

The man continued to stand up front by the register, and Griffin noted that he was quite tall, and not too bad looking if she were being honest. He was about the same age as she was and wore jeans and a navy-blue T-shirt, both of which fit him well.

He tried to wave down Alice, but she either ignored him or didn't see him, so he looked around the place as if searching for an empty spot in a packed room. After a few moments of some sort of internal debate, he decided on a two-top up against the wall, opposite Griffin and Marge's table. He settled in and inspected his menu but kept looking toward their booth, and

Griffin felt her cheeks redden. Something about him reminded her that she still had a giant princess-cut diamond in her left pocket. She'd managed to forget about it for a while, but now that she remembered, her internal struggle resumed over what to do about it.

"Did you like our beach house?" Marge looked at Griffin with wide, hopeful eyes.

"Who decorated it, Liberace?" Her grandmother's face sank with disappointment and Griffin felt bad that she'd gone too far. "It sure was … blue!" she said in a peppy tone. "Did y'all have a party last night? The place looked kind of a mess."

"A celebration," Marge said. "Although honestly, it's that messy all the time."

"Doesn't that drive you nuts?" Griffin asked.

Marge slapped her palms on the linoleum tabletop. "Darn tootin' it drives me nuts! Those women are slobs. I've never seen anything like it, and I looked after your grandpa for twenty-five years!"

Griffin had vague memories of her Grandpa Ziffy, from before G-ma divorced him for running off with the woman who looked after the produce at the local market. He'd made a comment about ripe bananas, the woman had responded with something about plums, and the rest was history, forever documented in the court records. Griffin didn't remember her G-pa being a slob, but G-ma still complained about him all the time.

"The stove was awfully clean though," Griffin said.

Marge looked happy again. "Yep! There's not a cook in the bunch except for me. I tell them to keep their filthy pizza box collection off my tidy stove. It's the only part of the whole house that I insist on keeping clean, except for my bedroom."

"Good for you for taking a stand," Griffin said. "What were you celebrating?"

"Smitty's an artist! She sold a couple of pieces yesterday."

"Oh, is she a painter or sculptor or what?"

G-ma cleared her throat. "Performance art."

Before Griffin could ask who Smitty was and how she had managed to sell a couple of pieces of performance art—maybe they were NFTs, she reasoned—her grandma changed the subject and started telling her about the senior's cruise.

"It was the most funnest thing ever! At first I was a little scared, see, on account of I was all by myself and didn't know anyone. Dinnertime was kind of a drag … You know how much I hate small talk. But on the second night I hooked up with the Blingsters at the Serve 'n Stuff Seafood Buffet, and life has been nonstop excitement ever since!"

"What the heck are Blingsters?"

"That's the name of the little gang my roommates are in. Oh, I mean group. Group, not gang. Yeah. Elva, Laverne, and Smitty. They call themselves the Bling Sisters, or the Blingsters for short."

"Are they really sisters?"

"Oh heck no, haha!" chirped Marge. "Sisters in crime maybe. Thick as thieves!"

"Weird name," Griffin said, taking a sip of her tea.

"Oh, I know," lamented G-ma. "But they're lovely gals and were great fun on the cruise. We got into all kinds of capers—I mean escapades—on the ship. And when we got back to Miami, they asked me if I wanted to stay longer. They lost their senior-senior member and said that I could move in with them since they had a spare bedroom."

"What's a senior-senior?"

"Yeah, she was the oldest, plus she'd been in the group the longest. Double senior whammy."

"What happened to her?"

G-ma looked down at her hands. "I'm not sure I should tell you."

Griffin had assumed that "losing" a senior-senior meant that said senior had passed on to the great retirement condo in the sky. But maybe not. The more G-ma spoke, the more questions Griffin had.

"It's okay," said Griffin in a reassuring tone. "You can tell me."

And whether or not she reported back to her parents with the answer remained to be seen.

"Well…" G-ma looked like she wanted to say something, but no explanation seemed to be forthcoming.

While she waited for her grandma to continue speaking, Griffin watched Alice place a tall glass full of a thick, green liquid in front of the good-looking man. A spoon stood straight up in the center of the green goo. He moved it aside, took a drink, and winced.

"Cop," said G-ma in a low voice.

"She was a cop?" Griffin asked and turned her gaze back to her grandmother.

"No," said Marge. "Him." She tilted her head toward the guy Griffin had been eyeing. Marge had been watching Griffin's ogling, and her facial expression indicated she also knew what Griffin had been thinking.

Griffin opened her mouth to defend herself but never got the chance to.

"Don't even think about it," said G-ma.

"I'm married!" Griffin exclaimed, sounding a little more defensive than she'd intended. She put her hand on her chest in mock astonishment and G-ma smiled.

"Eh, you could do better than him anyways."

"By him, do you mean that guy right there, or Brian?"

"Who's Brian?"

Griffin was about to get indignant until she caught the twinkle in her grandma's eye and realized she'd been pulling her leg. But still, for a moment she wondered if the remark meant that she could do better than a Florida cop they knew nothing about, or better than her husband, who was a money-loving accountant. She shook her head. "What's wrong with cops, anyway?" she asked. "I worked for the FBI you know. Hey, wait a minute! How do you know he's a cop?" Now she eyed her grandma with suspicion. Had she turned into a mob boss? Or a stool pigeon?

G-ma barked a laugh. "Ha! Just look at him! He screams

police. See his clothes? Too fancy for the beach. No one wears jeans here, or real shoes. And who else would be dumb enough to get a kelp smoothie at Moe's?"

Griffin didn't have an answer for that one.

Alice brought their food to the table. The cheeseburger smelled heavenly and even though Griffin didn't eat burgers but every few months, she was glad her grandma had ordered one for her after all. She took a bite and was in heaven.

"Great, right?" G-ma held a forkful of cheesy, hammy, egg scramble. Griffin only managed a nod since the speech part of her brain seemed to have been overtaken by the taste part of her brain. All thoughts of good-looking cops were momentarily forgotten.

"Well look who it is!" said a voice right next to their booth.

CHAPTER 5

It took great willpower, but Griffin turned her gaze away from her pile of onion rings to find a group of three women about G-ma's age had come into the diner and now stood next to their table. She recognized them all from the house—they were G-ma's roommates.

"Hello gals!" said Marge. "Let me introduce you to my granddaughter Griffin!"

Griffin tilted her head up to get a better look at them. While their faces seemed friendly to the untrained eye, she was getting a much different vibe. Perhaps it was because they looked down their noses at her, but they seemed to be scrutinizing her, and scrutinizing her hard.

G-ma pointed to the woman who had chatted up Griffin's boobs at the beach house. "Griffin, this is Laverne DePew."

Laverne wore elastic-waist jeans with a loose white summer sweater and white Keds. She looked like she had walked right off a sailboat. Her hair was pulled back, leaving a shelf of white bangs over her eyes, and she smiled that same benign smile at Griffin again.

"Hello dear," she said. Her left eye squinted slightly, and

Griffin knew right away that the woman was hiding something. But what? "You can call me Vern."

"Hi Vern," said Griffin. She smiled but made no move to shake the woman's hand. She'd tried that before and wasn't going to get snubbed a second time. Besides, Griffin's fingers were covered with burger and onion ring grease. She looked at Vern's hand though and noticed not one or two, but three diamond tennis bracelets on her wrist.

"And that over there is Elva Fiorini, or Big El to her pals." G-ma pointed to a woman who was as tall as a WNBA player and, if memory served, was the woman Griffin saw doing unspeakable things with someone who hopefully was at least a friend.

Big El had coppery hair and wore an all-white Adidas retro tracksuit. She had a brand-new pair of Stan Smiths on her feet, and huge rings on every finger. A few were sapphires set in platinum. One setting contained a giant ruby, and another ring featured an emerald. Her arms must have felt so heavy under the weight of all those rocks. Maybe that morning's bedroom activity had been a workout routine for all her jewelry wearing.

"Hi there, Griffin!" she said in an assertive voice with an Irish accent. "Did you like what you saw this morning?"

Griffin went rigid and began to turn red. All she could manage in response was a weak smile. G-ma gave her a questioning look, but Griffin shook her head which meant, *Let's not go there.*

"Okay … That's Daiyu Smith." G-ma pointed to the last woman, the one with the jet-black bob who'd taken a face-plant on her bed. She was the shortest of the group and wore a loose peasant blouse, culottes, and black suede flats. Gold earrings in the shape of Chinese dragons hung from her unusually large earlobes.

"Call me Smitty," she said, bowing. "Pleased to meet you." Her voice was so soft Griffin had to lean toward her to hear her over the incessant rattling of the ice machine.

All three women stood there looking so darned sweet. Almost. But not quite. Menacing was more like it.

"Thanks for watching out for my grandma," Griffin told them.

Vern laughed. "Oh sweetie, *she* watches out for *us*."

Griffin quirked an eyebrow at the cryptic response and glanced at her grandma, who had suddenly turned almost as green as the cop's smoothie. Speaking of which … She craned her head to try to see around Big El. The man was watching them out of the corner of his eye while wrestling with the spoon stuck in his kelp drink.

"We'll let you two catch up," Vern continued. She looked at Marge. "We'll see you later for canasta?"

"You betcha!" said Marge.

Vern gave Griffin a little wave and led her friends off to a table on the other side of the diner. Griffin couldn't be sure, but it looked as if Big El gave G-ma a stern look before walking off. G-ma nodded once.

"I didn't know you played canasta," said Griffin after the ladies had sat down. "I thought you loved bridge."

Marge picked up her fork. "Can't a woman try something new? What, you think once you hit seventy all your desire for fun shrivels up and falls off?"

Griffin recoiled. "I didn't mean it that way," she protested.

"Well what did you mean?" Marge stabbed at her eggs. "Honestly," she mumbled under her breath. "Some stuff might shrivel up and other stuff might almost fall off, but that doesn't mean I can't still have some fun."

Griffin felt bad for making her G-ma angry, but something felt really, really off. She leaned over her burger and said, "Okay G-ma, what's going on?"

"Nothing dear. Finish your onion rings."

Griffin and Marge ate in silence. Griffin kept looking at the cute guy, who had by now given up on his smoothie and was studying the table of bling-laden women. The ladies appeared to be deep in conversation. A very serious conversation by the looks of it.

"What's their deal?" Griffin asked.

"What do you mean?" asked Marge.

"Am I going to have to go over there and ask them?" She hated to give her grandmother an ultimatum, it sounded so … parental. But maybe Marge needed a little adult supervision these days.

"Shh!" hissed Marge. "Big El has right powerful hearing aids."

Griffin rolled her eyes. "Like anyone could hear us over that ice machine."

"That's one of the perks of coming here," said Marge. "No one can hear your conversation."

They continued to eat, and once Griffin had hit her grease quota for the next six months, she excused herself to go wash her hands in the bathroom. She stood at the sink and was pumping a second helping of hand soap into her palm when Smitty came in.

Griffin watched in the mirror as Smitty let the door close and stood in front of it, arms crossed. She was so small that Griffin could have sneezed and blown her out of the way. Yet she couldn't think of a time when she'd felt more intimidated in a women's restroom.

She turned off the water, reached for a paper towel, and smiled at Smitty as she dried her hands. Smitty's face remained expressionless until one side of her mouth twitched. It was almost imperceptible, but Griffin caught it and wondered if now might be a good time to try and recall some of those basic defensive moves they'd taught her at Quantico years ago.

Was Smitty blocking her path, or waiting for her to move away from the sink so she could use it? Hard to tell.

"We know," said Smitty in a low voice.

Griffin's mind raced as she tried to figure out her next move. "I'm sorry?"

"We know," Smitty repeated, arms still crossed. She looked Griffin over from head to toe. "About what you did."

"Oh, that." Griffin had no idea what the woman was talking about, but whatever it was, she started to feel really, really bad about it. And also a little scared. Then it hit her: maybe she did know what Smitty was talking about. She thought about reaching for the diamond—which was still in her pocket because she kept forgetting about it. But that would have been much too obvious.

"Yes, that," said Smitty. "How did you do it?"

Griffin thought back to that morning. "I stepped on it?"

Smitty cocked her head like she hadn't heard what Griffin had said.

"I mean, I just … felt around for something, and there it was."

Smitty frowned. "Could you do it again?"

Now Griffin was 100% lost. "Um, could you remind me what we're talking about?"

"Marge said that one time you found a whole lot of missing money for the government. Could you do that again, only in reverse?" Smitty glanced left, then right. "We could make it worth your while."

G-ma must have told her new friends about her biggest case. A year earlier, the Quintanilla Files made headlines when Griffin and her team recovered funds that had been invested offshore by a ring of high-end fountain pen smugglers. Okay, so the headlines were on their division's internal website, but she'd gotten an award and everything, so it totally counted as big news.

"You want my help hiding money from the government," said Griffin.

"Something like that, perhaps." Keeping her arms crossed, Smitty took three steps toward Griffin, about to violate her strict personal space rule. "The way we figure it, if you're good at finding things, you might be really good at hiding things."

Griffin's eyes darted around the bathroom, looking for an escape route. There wasn't one. "I'm kind of busy right now on another project," she said. "But how about I let you guys know when my schedule frees up, and we can talk then?"

Smitty nodded. "I suppose that's acceptable for now. But don't forget about us. The foot thing isn't working out."

Griffin wasn't sure what that was about but didn't want to hang around and ask for clarification. "Oh, I won't forget, I promise!" She nodded once in return, took a quick step to her left, and made a beeline for the door.

CHAPTER 6

"Griffy, you look like you've seen a ghost!" said Marge.

Griffin sat back down on her side of the booth. "No, just a miniature ninja."

"Oh, yeah. Smitty is kinda scary."

A woman walked up and placed their check on the table. She was tall, thin as a rail, and her face and hands looked like the parched, cracked dirt you saw in high-summer photos of Death Valley.

"How was everything?" the woman asked. Her voice sounded like sandpaper that had been sitting in that Death Valley sun for a month.

"Oh, hiya Little Moe," said Marge. "Everything was simply delish, wasn't it Griffy?"

This was Little Moe? Griffin had pictured someone more ... man-like. Okay, she'd pictured an actual man. But to her credit, Little Moe did sort of sound like one, so she hadn't been entirely off the mark.

"Yes, very good," Griffin agreed.

"Great, great," said Little Moe, nodding. "You gals need anything else?"

"No thank you," said Griffin.

"Actually, yes," said Marge. She looked around the diner, then motioned for Little Moe to lean in close. "See that feller over there with the kelp smoothie? Now don't everyone look all at once!"

Griffin stared at her empty plate because she knew who her grandma was talking about. Little Moe turned her head to look at the hot guy. "What about him?" she whispered.

"Could you please make him a cheeseburger and a side of onion rings? Griffin will give you money to cover it."

Griffin glowered at her, but G-ma didn't notice.

"Sure," said Little Moe. She smiled without showing any teeth —possibly because she didn't have any—and went back into the kitchen.

Perhaps Marge had forgotten that Griffin had recently been let go from her decent-paying job. She wasn't made of money, for cripes' sake! And her parents hadn't given her an expense account for this trip, only a vague promise to cover a night or two in a hotel plus the car rental and airfare. Griffin's husband did make good money at his accounting job with a private firm, but she always insisted on paying her own way as much as possible. However, paying for a stranger's lunch, even if he might be a cop, and a handsome one at that, was not in her budget.

"Stop glaring at me," said Marge. "He looks hungry."

Griffin and Marge went to the register by the door, and Griffin paid the bill out of what little cash she'd brought. As she put a few pennies in the tray on the counter, she noticed a fishbowl full of matchbooks for the diner and took one. On the back of the cover were written the words: *LITTLE MOE'S DINER, RAMONA PESCATELLI, OWNER. GOOD FOOD, YOU WILL LIKE.* She put the matches in her purse, and they left before the man's burger arrived, thereby avoiding the embarrassment of getting caught performing the diner version of sending a man a drink.

Once outside, Marge pointed down the street and they walked toward the ocean instead of going back to the car. At the end of the street, they bought ice cream from a little shop and then strolled out along the wooden pier.

"Little Moe seems interesting," said Griffin.

"Uh-huh," said Marge.

"Why 'little?' She didn't look all that little."

"Oh, that's just so's we don't get her mixed up with Big Moe."

"Any connection between the two?" Griffin asked.

Marge shrugged but said nothing.

"That guy must like his burger," Griffin said, changing the subject. "He didn't follow us."

"He wasn't there for you and me. He's watching the Blingsters."

Griffin wanted to point out that the man had arrived at the diner before the other ladies, but it seemed pointless. She knew her G-ma was a Blingster too. He was watching all of them.

The two women walked on, eating their ice cream. Griffin stopped a few times to look into the buckets that the fishermen had with them, but all she saw was smelly chunks of bait. No one had caught anything.

When Griffin finally got up her nerve, she made a declaration to her grandmother. "You need to come home with me," she said. In a fit of nervousness, she followed the words with an attempt to slurp up a bit of melted chocolate ice cream that dribbled over the side of her wax-paper cup. The ice cream shop had given them scoops the size of Texas.

"I can't," said Marge. "I'm kind of in the middle of something right now."

Griffin stopped walking and when Marge turned around to look at her, she gave her grandmother her best disapproving look, which she'd picked up from her own mother when she was fifteen. At the same time, the Texas-sized scoop of ice cream teetered, then fell out of the cup and onto the weathered boards of the pier.

"Oh Griffin," sighed Marge. "I see not much has changed."

Griffin huffed and rolled the ice cream back into the cup with her spoon and tossed it all in a nearby trash can. "This is not the time to analyze my childhood," she said. "Explain to me what's going on."

"I can't do that, sweetie." Pause. "Well, okay, I can explain a little, I guess."

"Spill it," said Griffin.

Marge laughed. "Haha! Like your ice cream, right? Oh Griffy, you have always been so funny."

But Griffin wasn't laughing. "I think I know the real reason you call them the Blingsters," she said.

"You do?"

"Yeah, sure. They were wearing enough gold to start their own jewelry store. They must be serious collectors, and rich too."

One of Marge's shoulders rose, which Griffin recognized as something her grandmother did when she was hedging. Like when Griffin was six and she'd asked G-ma where their family dog had gone. Her grandmother raised her shoulder and said that Barkus had left to become a bus driver in New York City. Then Griffin got caught trying to call a taxi so she could get to the airport to visit Barkus, and when she explained to everyone the reason for her unusual behavior, G-ma's shoulder had gone waaaaaay up.

"They don't exactly collect jewelry," said G-ma.

Griffin's stomach clenched. "G-ma, what have you gotten yourself into?"

"Let's just say that the ladies have some fun hobbies." She looked out at the water, squinting against the bright afternoon sun. Then she took another bite of her ice cream and continued down the pier.

Griffin had the distinct feeling that neither she nor her grandma would be heading back home on the evening flight. She got out her phone to look for a nearby hotel and to text her dad.

CHAPTER 7

Detective Roland Magnusson sat at the small table, hands wrapped around his giant kelp smoothie. Earlier that morning he had vowed to start eating better, right after scarfing down an Eggo FuFluffin from his favorite fast-food joint. The restaurant, a regional chain, had recently been sued for trademark infringement over the name of his beloved breakfast sandwich, but whatever they wanted to call it, it was damn good. He knew he needed to do better though—he was at that point in life where each meal choice had a greater impact. On everything.

That early-morning vow had resulted in his disastrous lunch selection. Surely there had to be some acceptable middle ground between total-crap-junk-food breakfast and total-crap-health-food lunch. He would go on a quest to find it.

A plate of food came into his line of sight and slid onto the table. A burger with onion rings. This was not quite what he'd had in mind.

"What's that?" he asked and looked up at the harbinger of doom, who seemed to have no teeth and skin like a rhinoceros.

"Burger and onion rings," she said in a tone that implied he was a little dim.

"I didn't order this," he said.

"Some ladies sent it over to you."

Roland looked around the restaurant but only saw the woman with her young son, who was now bouncing up and down in his seat singing something unintelligible, and the three decked-out seniors, each huddled over a plate stacked high with pancakes and bacon.

"They're gone now," the woman explained.

"Oh. Well, I guess I shouldn't let food go to waste," he said, pushing the smoothie away with one hand and pulling the burger closer with the other.

"What about the smoothie?"

"That doesn't count as food."

The woman left with the undrinkable drink and Roland tucked into the burger.

He thought about the two women who had sent him his new lunch. He remembered them well—one was older and part of the group of ladies he'd been watching. Marge Flanders. The other woman was younger and easy to look at, but he'd never seen her around before today. He would have remembered her, as she'd caught his eye.

Not many women caught his eye these days. Technically he was married, but that didn't mean other people couldn't still grab his attention from time to time, right? Who was he kidding. He was a terrible husband. He would never cheat, but he also didn't seem to have the energy to try very hard at being married anymore. To be fair, neither did his wife.

Roland was about halfway through his burger when the senior ladies began to make signs they were going to leave soon. They all leaned back in their chairs, and the red-haired one, Elva, patted her stomach. One of them let rip a loud burp, but he couldn't tell which one. Daiyu, who always reminded him of a tiny, deadly ninja, went to the register to pay the check and the rest of them stood to leave as well.

Sadly, there was no time to ask for a to-go box for his food, so half a burger and a few onion rings would have to hold him over until he could find some fruit or a salad or something, because he needed to follow these unusual women.

He'd been watching them from a distance for a few weeks, after stumbling upon a piece of information while working on a murder investigation. It had been one of those down-the-rabbit-hole situations. The ladies ended up not being connected to the murder, but a fact in the case piqued his curiosity, and here he was. Robbery wasn't his beat, but it was a nice change of pace from his usual, more depressing workload.

He'd done a little checking up on the women. Three of them had criminal records going as far back as fifty years. Their crimes ran the gamut from petty theft to embezzlement, and all three had served time. But their records had been clean for the last two decades.

He had also followed each of them, tailing the one named Elva to a Cuban bakery, and Laverne to the mall. Twice he'd followed Marge and Daiyu Smith to the gym, where Daiyu alternated between teaching Marge basic fighting skills, and taking kickboxing classes while Marge got massages.

So far, Roland hadn't been able to come up with a scrap of evidence that indicated they were doing anything outside the law. But he had that feeling, that detective instinct. Something was fishy. Plus, if he was investigating them, it meant less time at home, which lately had been a good thing. His wife Christina never complained about his absence, and when he was home, she always seemed angry with him. Who'd want to go home to that?

Roland watched the three ladies leave the diner and walk toward their car, a little BMW X3. The ninja got in behind the wheel and peeled out of the lot. He tossed some money on the table for his terrible smoothie and ran out the door to follow them.

For fifteen minutes Roland tailed the BMW, until it stopped in front of a nondescript three-story office building and idled at the curb. The white-haired woman, Laverne, got out of the back seat and reached back inside the car, pulled out a black tote bag, and headed into the building.

Interesting! Perhaps this was a warehouse of some sort, or a front for their nefarious undertakings. The BMW began to pull away from the curb, and Roland had to make a quick decision—follow the car or stay and watch. He never had a chance to decide because the ninja was too fast, and the black BMW disappeared into traffic. He would stay.

Recently the women's behavior had become stranger, if that were possible, for they were a mighty strange bunch to begin with. They kept odd hours and seemed to have a lot of visitors to their beach house. His gut instinct told him things were about to get interesting, and his intuition was right most of the time. Why, just three months before, he'd received a special commendation from the department for solving a high-profile dolphin theft from the home of a national political figure who resided in Palm Beach —at least according to his tax return. Roland's hunch pointed him toward the theory that the politician had faked the theft for publicity and so he could file a claim against his home insurance. He'd been right.

After five minutes, Roland thought about getting out of the car and looking around a bit. Maybe he'd walk past the front door, but there was the risk that the woman might see him, and he'd be recognized. If he went around the back, he might miss her departure. It was times like this he wished the whole thing was an official investigation so he could get some help. But when he'd approached his captain with information about a possible senior-citizen theft ring, his boss had thought he was nuts and his partner had suggested a long vacation.

Roland decided to go have a look around. He got out of his car and, with his hands in his pockets, walked toward the building and read the plaque by the door as he went by. The first two floors were occupied by a group of podiatrists and the third line on the sign, which should have shown who was on the top floor, was blank. *Bingo.* He went back to his car and got comfortable, wishing he had the other half of his free burger, which had been quite good. He'd have to go back sometime and have a whole one. With a salad of course.

After twenty minutes, Laverne came out of the building with a big white bandage on her right foot and used a cane to make her way to the curb. Within seconds, the BMW pulled up and she got in, and they left.

Roland stayed put and pondered the situation. Either the bandage had been an elaborate cover, in which case they were being very careful (or might even know they were being watched), or she really had gone into the podiatrist for something. He wished he could waltz into the doctor's office and ask about her, but thanks to those damn HIPAA rules and all that privacy junk, that was a nonstarter.

One thing he could do, however, was check out the third floor. He clipped his badge to his waist and for good measure, put his shoulder holster back on.

The elevator seemed too obvious, so he took the stairs. As he climbed, he was reminded of his poor food choices and vowed once again to eat better, as well as hit the gym a little more often. On the third floor, a flight of stairs continued up to the roof of the building, but Roland crept toward the door leading to the main office space. He opened it an inch and peered in.

It wasn't what he'd expected. Not that he was sure exactly what he'd expected—maybe an empty space with no drywall or finishings of any kind? Or maybe nondescript offices, all empty. In either case he hoped he'd be able to search around for stolen goods. But he found neither of those scenarios.

Instead, he was peering into a fancy lobby. The huge, front-facing desk sported a marble top, and large plants lined the wall behind the desk space. It all looked very upscale, Roland thought.

There was no signage anywhere to indicate what the business was. A single hallway led away from the lobby, but he couldn't see anything beyond a few feet down the passageway. Now that he was looking at the place, it seemed unlikely that Laverne

DePew had come up here. But in the name of thoroughness, he would go in and see what was what.

A young woman with long flowing brown hair sat at the front desk, and Roland entered the lobby and approached her. She was smartly dressed in a low-cut silk blouse and a very short skirt, that he happened to notice without meaning to.

"Hello, I'd like to talk to whoever's in charge here," he said, trying not to sound like a cop.

She looked at him from head to toe, and a smile spread across her face. "Okay," she said in a tone that hinted there might be an invitation in there somewhere. She bent over her phone, revealing even more cleavage, and spoke into the phone's intercom. "Juan, someone's here to see you."

"Send them to the conference room," a man barked through the speaker in a heavy Latin accent.

"This way," she said to Roland. She stood up and walked him down the hallway to a glassed-in conference room. "Wait in there." She gave him that smile again as he entered. She closed the door, and he watched through the glass as she sauntered back to the lobby.

The room was bare save for one long table with a phone, a boom box, and a group of chairs on one end. No art on the walls, no sign with a company name. Roland was still stumped.

"There you are. You're late!" A short man with jet-black hair rushed into the room and slammed the door behind him. He wore a colorful silk shirt with an ascot, beige linen pants, and no shoes or socks.

"What?" said Roland.

"You're cute so I'll let it slide," the man said.

"Are you in charge here?" asked Roland.

"You bet your bippie! I make alllll the decisions. Now take off your clothes."

"What?" said Roland again.

"Go on! Take them off." He crossed his arms and tapped his foot in mock consternation.

"I think there's been a mistake," said Roland. He pointed to the badge on his hip. "Are you Juan?"

"Omigod, that's perrrrfect!" said the man. "A cop routine, I love it! Do you have a hat too? Maybe a … night*stick*?" Then he saw Roland's weapon and fanned himself. "Oh my. This just keeps getting better and better. A super-hot cop with his own gun. Oh, this will be good. Wait a minute!" He ran over to the boom box and pressed play on the tape deck. Def Leppard's "Pour Some Sugar on Me" blared through the room. "Okay, go!" he yelled.

Roland was thoroughly confused. "Exactly what kind of business is this?" he asked over the music.

Ten minutes later, Roland had explained to the owner of the stripper agency that he was not there looking for a job, but okay, thank you, he would keep the man's card and call if he changed his mind. He left the office building convinced that Laverne had simply gotten a bunion removed.

CHAPTER 8

By the time Griffin located a hotel she could afford, she was looking at a Travel Lodge in Florida City. But her G-ma insisted on using her senior discount and springing for a suite at some super-fancy place that had both the words "Resort" *and* "Spa" in the name. She also told Griffin to take the Mercedes for the evening after Griffin had expressed so much admiration for her grandmother's car. Griffin wasn't one to argue.

However, Marge refused to stay at the hotel with her, demanding to be dropped off back at her beach house. The rental car stayed in the carport, and Griffin left with the Mercedes but not her grandma. Before leaving, Griffin got Marge to agree to meet the following day for a drive through the Keys.

The next morning, Griffin enjoyed a leisurely breakfast on the balcony of her swanky hotel room. She was on the second floor and had a prime view of the ocean. At first she almost wished that Brian were there to enjoy it with her. It could have been a nice stand-in for the Hawaii vacation he kept promising her. But by the end of her meal, she wasn't so sure it would have been nicer to have him there. He'd really been a pill lately. Regardless, perhaps she should text him. He hadn't reached out to her since she'd arrived, to see how she was doing. Disappointing.

She sent him a quick good morning text … but never heard back. She'd try again later, she decided.

As she got dressed to leave, Griffin had the presence of mind to put the giant diamond in the hotel room's safe, shoved into a pair of sport socks (like it wouldn't be weird or obvious to find sport socks in a safe). When she'd first checked in, she had tucked the rock into her suitcase, folded inside her UCLA sweatshirt—a gift from her other grandma, Delphine, who lived in Southern California and was an alum—but then thought better of it. Surely the safe would be the best place to leave the gemstone while she was gone.

She still didn't know why she'd taken it, or what she was going to do with it. If she gave it back at this point, it would look strange. She would get asked why she had kept it so long before returning it. And who would she give it to? She could give it to Marge, who would probably cover for her and say she'd found it in the beach house living room, but Griffin didn't want to accidentally get her grandma in trouble. If she quietly held onto it, it could still be anywhere, right? Just … lost. Unless Vern had seen her pick it out of the ocean of blue carpet and hadn't said anything. She decided to give it more thought some other time.

A half hour later, she picked up Marge from the beach house, and they drove down Highway 1 with the moon roof of the beautiful German car open to the Florida elements: sun, sun, and more sun.

They drove in silence for a long stretch of highway, with Marge only chatting when she saw something that caught her interest enough to comment on, which wasn't that often. The scenery from the car was beautiful at times, and Griffin felt she was getting her fill of ocean quality time—compared to being in Fort Worth, anyway.

Neither of them knew much about the area. Griffin had never been to Florida before and as far as she knew, neither had Marge. But Griffin was starting to realize that her grandma might be leading a much more interesting life than any of them suspected.

Was Marge's silence because she was stressed about something, or did she have another Natty Light hangover?

Griffin's own silence was due to stress—she wasn't sure if she was more concerned about the diamond or the mysterious situation her G-ma had gotten herself into. Frankly, it was a toss-up.

The women's silence didn't get in the way of their appetites, however, and around noon they stopped for lunch at a seafood restaurant overlooking the sparkling Atlantic Ocean. They didn't want to take a chance on a completely unknown place, so Griffin had her grandma check the online reviews before they went in. The restaurant, which looked more like a shack, had tons of four- and five-star ratings and it turned out that the reviewer who went by the handle *PunkinSpice82* was dead on—the lobster was terrific.

They sat outside at a wooden picnic table under a large tree whose branches hung over their heads and provided shade from the midday sun. They were finishing their iced teas and Griffin had been waiting for Marge to tell her the real story behind the sorority beach house she was living in, but so far, her grandma hadn't said a word.

"Your friends are into some questionable shit, aren't they," Griffin said.

"Griffin! Watch your language." Marge looked around to make sure no one had overheard her granddaughter's potty mouth, which elicited an eye roll from said granddaughter. "But, well … Yes, they are."

"Which means that you're involved in that sh—"

"One more word like that and I'm calling your mother."

"I'm not eight anymore, G-ma. And you can try to switch the subject as often as you want, but it doesn't change the fact that something is very off here."

Marge hung her head and sighed with resignation, but said nothing.

Griffin crossed her arms. "Fine. You don't need to give me details, but we do need to leave Florida tonight."

"I can't," Marge said. "I'm on a new canasta team! We have a big game coming up real soon and I can't up and leave them right now."

"Sure you can. Your 'canasta team' will do fine without you." Griffin used air quotes on the canasta team part because she could smell an innocent-sounding cover story standing in for something sketchy from a mile away.

"No," said Marge. "I'm not leaving."

"So it's not that you can't leave, it's more that you won't leave?"

Marge didn't answer. Oh good lord, thought Griffin. Her grandma was living a life of crime and enjoying it.

"But I just got a new Mercedes!" Marge whined, as if reading Griffin's thoughts.

Griffin loved her grandma dearly, but she still wanted to bonk the woman's head into the picnic table. "Are you nuts?"

"Maybe," said Marge, and let out a loud burp, followed by a giggle.

"I don't get it," said Griffin.

"Get what, Griffy?"

"It's like I don't know who you are anymore! Some outrageous, over the top crazy woman is inhabiting my G-ma's body."

Marge slurped more tea.

"Did something happen on the cruise to cause this change? Or maybe even something before that? Is anything wrong?" Griffin could hear the desperation in her own voice. It wasn't flattering, but she was at her wit's end.

"Look," said Marge, pushing her drink away. "Maybe you'll understand when you get to be my age."

"Doubtful," mumbled Griffin.

"What was that?"

"I don't know, G-ma. This is all so weird. I'm not sure it suits you."

"Are you kidding?" she yelled. "It suits me great! Look at me, I look fabulous!" She pointed to her jumpsuit, which featured a brown, white, and gold Hawaiian floral print. The gold jewelry around her neck and on her wrists complemented the colors of her outfit to a T. Griffin had to agree, she looked fabulous.

"And I feel fabulous too! Doesn't suit me? Pffft!"

"But—"

"And my car!" said Marge. "Just look at him!" She pointed to the Mercedes, gleaming in the sunlight, and looking badass and beautiful, all at the same time.

"Him?" asked Griffin.

"I named him Otto," said Marge in a breathy, lovestruck voice.

Griffin sighed. "Okay."

"Anyway, I probably have to get back." Marge pulled a brand-new iPhone in a rhinestone case out of her Kate Spade purse and checked the time. "Oh shit!"

That elicited another eye roll from Griffin. "What now, a hair appointment?"

"No, canasta club! We have a strategy session this afternoon. Come on, let's go! I can just make it if we put the pedal to the metal. I'm driving. You drive like an old lady." She held out her hand and Griffin dropped the keys into her palm with more than a little hesitation.

That could have been one of the worst mistakes Griffin had ever made in her life. But as luck would have it, they made it back safe and sound, only having cut off four cars and a truck, and narrowly missing one bus. Marge dropped Griffin off at the entrance to the resort since it was on the way to her house.

"Go for a swim or get a massage," said Marge. "I hear those hot rock thingies are great. Remember, it's all on me, so have a good time, okay? I'll call you later and maybe we'll do an early dinner. The Down Home Buffet and Car Wash has a great senior special from four to four-thirty."

Griffin watched her grandma peel out down the street. She was going to need new tires pretty soon.

CHAPTER 9

No sooner had Marge left than Griffin realized she had no car—her rental was still at the beach house. Technically she didn't need one, since she'd told her grandma that she would stay at the resort all afternoon, but still. She liked to have options. In fact, she decided she would forgo the massage and opt for checking up on her G-ma instead. And for that she would need her car. Now she had to spend more money to call a ride to pick her up and take her back to the beach.

She had a twenty-minute wait, so she hung out in the lobby, checking email on her phone. Brian still hadn't texted back. Wasn't that sort of weird? Lately she'd had a strange feeling that he was cheating on her, but she had no proof. She was probably just stressed from losing her job, she reasoned, and the fact that they were in the middle of buying a new house only added to the feeling. Maybe he was busy organizing their upcoming move. She tried to text him again.

Griffin: *Hey, how's it going?*

Brilliant conversation, Griffin.

Griffin: *Have you and Shelby worked out the closing details?*

No answer from Brian.

Maybe he was working out the loan closing details right that minute with their realtor, Shelby Wafer. Griffin grimaced when she thought about Shelby. Approximately 64% of the woman's body parts looked surgically enhanced, and Griffin couldn't tell if the woman was faking being stupid, or if she did in fact have the IQ of a train caboose. But she was blond and cute, and Brian had insisted she was the best person for them to work with.

On second thought, Griffin hoped Brian was not working with Shelby on the closing right then.

She hadn't wanted to buy a new house; nothing was wrong with the one they were in. The new one that Brian had found with the real estate agent was beautiful, to be sure, but too far out of Griffin's comfort zone as far as the price was concerned. Plus it was way over the top, kind of McMansiony. It was in a neighborhood where all the houses looked the same and were about three feet apart from each other. Why did the two of them need matching home offices and a study? And a pool house? Please. In Griffin's opinion, living at or below one's means was the only way to get ahead, but Brian always liked to live large. They were one of those couples who often fought about money.

So sure, that nagging feeling she had was probably nothing more than stress.

Griffin looked up from her phone when the app informed her that her driver was almost to the resort. It was then she noticed a man sitting in a late 2010s Crown Victoria parked in the lot across from the hotel entrance. He looked a lot like the guy who'd attempted to drink a kelp smoothie at Little Moe's the day before. The man ducked down behind the steering wheel before Griffin could get a better look at him.

Her ride showed up right then, and thankfully the driver was much better at navigating traffic than her grandmother had been.

As the car slowed down and approached the beach house, Griffin spied a group of ladies standing around by the carport. Marge's Mercedes had her rental car boxed in.

"Can you stop here?" Griffin asked when they were about five houses away.

The driver complied and let her out, and then drove away. Griffin crouched behind a parked car to watch the Blingsters. It looked like they were having an interesting conversation. Big El waved her arms around, and suddenly bent her knees to crouch like a tiger. Marge doubled over with laughter and Smitty managed a faint smile. After what Griffin had seen going on in Big El's bedroom the day before, she was thankful she couldn't hear the conversation. Lord only knew what those flailing arms were meant to convey.

She heard a car approaching behind her and turned to look. It was the same car from the resort—that kelp-smoothie-drinking cop was following her! What had *she* done? Besides take that diamond. But he couldn't know about that. At least she was pretty sure, but this wasn't the time to worry about it. He pulled into a spot a few houses down and killed his engine.

Griffin began to fret. She needed to watch what was happening up ahead at the beach house, but that might leave her open if the man in the car decided to sneak up on her. He was a cop though—or so her grandma said. But what if he wasn't a cop? Again she kicked herself for not remembering more from her defensive training. She thought about pulling her keys out of her purse and holding them so she could stab him if he came up behind her, but it would probably take her five minutes to find the keys in her purse and by then it would be too late.

Before she could debate any further, the ladies in the carport all laughed again one last time as they piled into two cars. The Mercedes and the BMW backed out of the carport, leaving Griffin's rental car free. Once they were out of sight, she ran to her car, got in, and took off after them. Her tail would have to fend for himself—her grandma's safety was her main concern.

CHAPTER 10

Griffin followed the Blingsters and the cop followed Griffin. They all ended up at a Cheesecake Factory in Palmetto Bay.

The ladies entered a meeting room at the back of the restaurant. Once it was safe, Griffin went to the bar, which offered a clear view of the private dining area. They'd left the door open and from the counter, Griffin could see into the room and keep an eye on them. She suspected she might be able to hear what they were saying if she passed by on her way to the bathroom at a slow enough pace.

The cop took a seat at the other end of the bar, and Griffin had the bartender serve him a Budweiser. If he was trying to be discreet, he was doing a lousy job. He looked at her when the server placed the beer in front of him and Griffin raised her water glass in greeting, which he must have taken as an invitation to join her because over he came.

They sat in silence for a few minutes—the cop sipping his beer, Griffin sipping her water.

"For future reference, I like imports," he said, not taking his eyes off the polished wood counter.

"You're welcome," said Griffin. "I figured you must work up a real thirst tailing people all day."

"You have no idea," he said.

A basketball game played on a TV behind the bar; the Heat was losing to the Orlando Magic. They both watched it, although Griffin couldn't care less.

"Do I want to know what your role is in all this?" he asked her.

Griffin looked at him now. "Do *I* want to know *your* role?"

"Fair enough."

The whole situation had Griffin on edge. Trying to keep up with her grandma's Mercedes had proven challenging—the woman was a lead foot! Also, sitting with a man who spied on old ladies stressed her out. Usually she did okay under pressure, but she'd never had to surveil her own grandma before. This was not what she'd signed up for when she had told her dad she would go to Florida.

"Watch my purse," Griffin said, and she placed her bag on the bar and headed to the restroom. Only when she was halfway there did she realize what a stupid, stupid move that had been. A dumb sports metaphor came to mind, something about being off her game … or was it there's no I in team? In any case, she prayed she wouldn't regret her rookie move any more than she already did. Hopefully he truly was a cop and not a thief. Or worse. She didn't have the diamond with her, so that was lucky, but having her driver's license and credit cards stolen would be bad indeed.

Griffin slowed her pace as she approached the open door of the meeting room and walked by as leisurely as she could without stopping. She prayed none of the ladies would notice her. All four of them sat hunched over a table, looking at a big piece of paper. It looked like it might have been a set of blueprints.

To her disappointment, it turned out she couldn't hear what the women were talking about. She did catch a few words, something about *practice run* and *diversion,* and possibly the word *intel* was thrown around.

She had never played canasta, but none of what she saw or heard seemed to have anything to do with playing cards.

Griffin was so focused on the activity in the room that she almost bumped into a server carrying a large tray of fried foods, which he was about to take in to the Blingsters. It looked like high cholesterol was not on their list of concerns.

"Sorry," she said to the server, who only glared at her before entering the meeting room.

When Griffin made it back to the bar and sat down in front of her water glass and purse, her new friend asked, "Where did you go?"

"To the bathroom, not that it's any of your business," she snapped.

"It's just that you didn't actually go to the bathroom."

"Oh." Griffin opened her purse and began to search through it, pretending to look for something. Thank goodness, nothing seemed to be missing. What a gentleman. She pulled out a pen and acted like she wanted to write something but couldn't find a piece of paper. She shrugged and pretended to change her mind and shoved the pen back in her bag. She was sure she had fooled exactly no one.

"Look," he said. He scooted his barstool closer to hers, and it made a horrible noise as it scraped along the sticky tile floor. "I don't know who you are or how you're involved in all of this, but for your own sake, you should take off right now and not look back."

"Hi, I'm Griffin Beckett." She stuck out her hand for him to shake.

That stopped him cold for a few seconds, but he recovered well and took her hand while giving her a nice smile. "Roland Magnusson." His hand felt warm, which was nice. But her own hand was sweaty, which wasn't so nice.

"Come here often, Rolly?"

"No one calls me Rolly. And no, I don't. You?"

Griffin motioned for the bartender to come back over, and when he did, she pushed the half-empty glass of Budweiser toward him. "Please dispose of this bilge water. Rolly will take whatever German beer you have on tap. I'll have the same. On him."

The bartender nodded and moved off to get their drinks.

"Bilge water?" asked Roland.

"I share your disdain for domestics." It all tasted like bilge water to her, but he didn't have to know that.

He nodded thoughtfully. "What makes you think I'm going to pay for your beer?"

"Because it's the least you can do after I bought you that burger yesterday."

"Right. Thanks for that," he said. "It was really good. Beat the pants off that damn smoothie."

"You're welcome," said Griffin, and she smiled. "The look on your face when you took that first sip was priceless."

"Talk about bilge water," he said, and smiled.

The bartender brought their beers and out of curiosity, Griffin asked Roland if his kelp smoothie at Moe's had gotten any better after that first taste. It turned out that G-ma had in fact saved her from a very bad decision.

They drank their beers and made pointless small talk for a while. Every time Roland tried to ask her a personal question, she deflected it with a question of her own or a trip to the bathroom, which she ended up visiting three more times (remembering to take her purse with her on all three occasions).

From what Griffin could tell, the Blingsters were making some sort of important plan that included not only blueprints, but also a few maps (who even used paper maps anymore?) and a whole bunch of fried appetizers, plus an entire chocolate raspberry cheesecake.

The pit of Griffin's stomach was filled with worry, and it was not a good feeling. When she sat back down next to Roland after her third walkabout, she sighed with frustration.

"You should probably see a doctor about your small bladder," he said.

"Are you married?" she asked.

"What?"

"I figured that if we're going to get up close and personal with each other, I should at least find out if you're married."

"Looking at that rock on your finger, I take it you are," he said, his eyes not leaving the beer glass in front of him. "And yes, I'm married too."

Griffin thought she heard a bit of regret in his voice. Maybe just as much regret as she was feeling about the subject. Then she felt bad about feeling regretful.

She stared at the ring on her finger and thought about Brian. She wondered what he was doing right then. A little voice in the back of her head told her no, she did not want to know.

At that exact moment, her phone rang from deep inside her bag. It took her several attempts to find it, as it was in its own special pocket in the inner lining of her purse, right where it was supposed to be, but not where she thought to look. She pulled it out and answered before looking to see who it was, for fear of missing the call.

"Hello?"

"Babe."

"Oh. Hi Brian. One sec." She lowered the phone to her side and turned to Roland. "Excuse me, I have to take this." He waved a hand her way and continued staring at his beer.

Griffin took her purse and began to leave the restaurant for the parking lot, where she could hear a little better. "What's up? How are you?" she asked as she walked.

"Where are you, babe?" he asked, ignoring her question.

She hated it when he called her babe. Usually nothing good followed that word. "I'm in Florida City. At a Cheesecake Factory. It's complicated."

"Sounds like it."

Griffin stepped outside into the humid afternoon sunshine. "Yeah, you wouldn't believe it! There's some seriously weird stuff going on down here."

"Uh-huh. I thought you were coming home today."

"Honestly, at this point, I don't know when I'll be back." Brian didn't say anything, and Griffin knew something wasn't right. "What's wrong?"

"I was sort of hoping you'd be home tonight, so I could tell you this in person, but maybe it's better this way."

"Why, so I don't punch you in the face?"

Brian let out his signature nervous laugh and Griffin braced for impact.

"You don't even know what I'm going to say!" he said.

But Griffin knew. "Get on with it."

"We got an offer on our house yesterday, and I took it."

That wasn't so bad, so that must not be all of it. "But we don't have any place to move into—the new house isn't ready yet."

"Um, about that. See, I'm going to move in with Shelby, she has an apartment in Southlake. When I close on the new place, she and I will move in there."

Griffin's stomach seemed to puddle on the hot asphalt around her feet. "Oh."

"Yeah, and I've arranged to have all your stuff put in storage. They're coming tomorrow to pick it up. You know, one of those pod things."

"What?" was all Griffin could manage to say.

"Don't worry, I'll pay for the setup fee and the first three months."

"I see."

"I'm real sorry, Griff. It's just, well, you and I don't have much in common. We never did, I guess. And lately..." He didn't finish the sentence, and he didn't have to. She knew what he meant.

It was like having her heart ripped out through the 5G network so he could stomp on it in their kitchen in Fort Worth. And yet she didn't feel like speaking up or protesting. There was some truth in what he was saying. However, he'd also just admitted he'd been sleeping with their real estate agent.

"Babe?" he asked.

"You and Shelby," she said. It wasn't a question.

"Oh yeah, right. It's funny, me and her have a lot in common!"

I bet, thought Griffin. "Uh-huh. Wait, how come we have to be out of the house so soon if it only sold this week?"

"Well..."

It kept getting better and better. "You didn't just sell the house," she said. And then she hung up on him.

CHAPTER 11

The whole world looked different to Griffin once she hung up on her husband. She stood in the parking lot of the Cheesecake Factory in Palmetto Bay feeling detached from her surroundings, and from Brian. Had she ever felt all that attached to him in the first place though? The sting of betrayal was the worst part, but that was not very surprising either. None of it seemed surprising. Which was sad.

Sad, mad, detached, then mad again—everything cycled through her thoughts until it all became a jumble. What should she do next? She didn't feel like crying, she knew that much. If anything, she felt more like breaking something, but that would be inappropriate and there was nothing handy nearby that wouldn't involve explaining herself to an insurance company.

No, she should look at what was going on right in front of her. Her grandma seemed to be in some seriously deep water, and she needed to focus on that. She would go back in the restaurant to keep an eye on Marge, and deal with Brian and his crap later.

She took that proverbial deep breath and made her way back into the restaurant, where Roland still sat at the bar, only now he was staring at a glass of water instead of a beer.

"Everything okay?" he asked as she sat down.

"No."

"Oh," he said, sounding surprised.

Because you were always supposed to lie and say yes when someone asked you that question. She felt his eyes on her and when she turned his way, he looked concerned.

"It's fine," she finally said, deciding to stick to conventional conversation rules.

Roland gave his silent approval of that plan.

"Did I miss anything?" she asked, looking toward the meeting room. The door was still open, and the ladies were no longer studying blueprints. Instead, each of them were focused on eating some kind of chocolatey dessert.

"They ordered another cheesecake," he informed her. "They must have arteries like steel pipes."

"I think they're just living it up," said Griffin in a sudden burst of empathy. "What have they got to lose?"

"Hmm." Roland looked pensive.

"Rolly, why are you following these little old ladies?"

"I'm not at liberty to say," he answered, not missing a beat. "And don't call me that."

"Cut the crap," Griffin said, and their eyes met. He looked serious, but he was probably someone who looked serious all the time.

"Okay," he said but took a drink of water before continuing, making her wait. "Three of those women are dangerous criminals. I've been following them for a while now, but I haven't been able to pin anything on them. It's just a matter of time though."

Griffin wondered if his one beer had gone to his head since he was being so forthcoming now. Because he didn't seem like the sharing type. And also, what he said seemed preposterous.

"Oh come on," Griffin said, followed by a laugh intended to show him how ridiculous she thought he was being. "They're ancient! How dangerous could they be?" She shook her head at the thought.

"They've got criminal records as long as your arm," he said.

They both looked at her cardigan-clad arm and she wiggled her fingers. Then he pointed a thumb at the private room. "And that one in the culottes? She may look frail, but she'll break every bone in your body given half a chance."

Griffin knew he was talking about Smitty. The woman might have been a little scary, but it still didn't all compute. "Please," she said.

"The fourth one, the one in the jumpsuit, I don't know about her. She's new. She's either an innocent bystander whom they've pulled into their orbit, or she's a brilliant mastermind whom they've brought in as their new leader."

A wave of dread washed over Griffin; he was talking about her G-ma. Based on what she had seen since she'd arrived in Florida, she wasn't sure which of Rolly's guesses were correct. But seriously. Smitty had to be in her late seventies, Big El too. Whatever they were doing in there with blueprints and maps had to be something benign, like maybe some kind of prank to remind them of their lost youths. Maybe they were planning to sneak into a retirement village and kidnap one of their friends to take them out to breakfast in their pajamas, like the popular kids did in high school. Not that Griffin was ever popular enough to have that happen to her personally, but she'd seen it in movies.

"So is one of those women in there your mom?" he asked.

The disappointment at once again being mistaken for G-ma's daughter turned to low-level anger.

"Yeah," she said. "And I have to leave soon to pick up my grandkids from school."

His head snapped in her direction.

Griffin shook her head. "No, Rolly. My mother is not in there."

"Why not just tell me what your involvement is here? You know I could easily go back to the station and look you up. I took a photo of your driver's license when you left me in charge of your purse."

"Aw crap," said Griffin. "I forgot about that." She was

embarrassed to think she had ever worked for the FBI. No wonder they fired her.

"So?"

"That fourth member you were talking about, in the jumpsuit. She's my grandma. My parents sent me here to try to take her back to Oklahoma."

"But you live in Fort Worth," he observed.

"Very astute. Like you live near your parents?"

"Oh hell no," he said. "I moved halfway across the country as soon as I got my degree."

"There you go. Yes, I live in Fort Worth. For now, anyway. My G-ma lives down the street from my parents in Enid. I guess you have our whole family history now."

"Seems that way," he said. "Griffin R. Beckett, thirty-two, Fort Worth resident ... for now, she says. Her grandmother is a suspected thief, and she spends her downtime talking with a handsome local police detective."

Griffin looked at him with fake reverence. "And this is Florida's tax dollars hard at work."

"Not really," said Roland. "I'm working this one on my own time. These ladies are kind of like my hobby."

"I bet your wife likes that," said Griffin. She regretted it as soon as she said it, but she was feeling bitter, so too bad.

He didn't say anything for a few beats, then changed the subject. "What did you mean you live in Texas 'for now'?"

"Oh, nothing. I ... I don't want to talk about it." She couldn't help but notice that Brian hadn't tried to call her back after she hung up on him. The next time she heard from him would probably be through a divorce attorney.

Roland nodded. "I get that."

Griffin eyed the meeting room. "They're on the move."

Roland looked toward the meeting room too, and then back at the basketball game on the TV.

She got off her barstool and started searching for her wallet but couldn't find what purse pocket she had slid it into earlier. Before she could locate it, Roland spoke.

"I've got the bill, remember? My turn."

She looked up from her bag and their gazes met. For a split second, it was as if her own loneliness was reflected back to her in his eyes. But then the moment passed, and his look grew dark. His usual countenance, it seemed.

"Right, thanks." She smiled and waited for him to stand up too, but he didn't seem to be getting ready to leave. "Aren't you coming? They're heading out to the parking lot."

"No, I think I'm done for the day."

"But what if they, uh, try something?"

He squinted at her as if sizing her up. "I'm sure you can handle it."

"Huh. Okay." She put her purse over her shoulder but stayed standing there, facing the bar.

"Are you sure you're all right?" he asked her.

"I think so, yeah."

"Be careful, okay? Those women are extremely dangerous."

She looked at him, and his brown eyes seemed even darker now. She nodded once and left.

CHAPTER 12

When the four ladies left the Cheesecake Factory, Roland decided to take a break from following them. A little distance wouldn't hurt, at least for a little while. He could tell that the seniors were close to taking action. It would be easy to think of another theft as a bad thing, but as far as he was concerned, it would be an opportunity for them to slip up. And he'd be there to catch them in the act when they did. It just required some patience on his part.

He also considered following his new friend Griffin since he still wasn't sure what her angle was. Sure, she said she was there to take her grandmother back to Oklahoma, but he'd been trained to be doubtful. In the courtroom it was innocent until proven guilty, but in his experience, it was best to opt for suspicious until proven clear.

It wasn't late by any stretch, but most people would be headed home soon. It was the perfect time to go back into the office to catch up on paperwork.

At least that was his official rationalization, and it was partly true.

"Working late again, huh Magnusson?" The voice of his boss, Captain Perez, sounded from the doorway of his office, causing

Roland to look up from his desk. "Old ladies still taking up all your free time? I hope you've been working out so you can keep up with 'em."

He'd been the butt of countless jokes around the office since word got out that he was doing a little sleuthing on the side and that his pet project happened to involve a bunch of septuagenarians. But he'd show them … as soon as he could come up with something concrete, which had proven difficult so far.

"I think I can keep up just fine," Roland said.

"That's not what your wife says," retorted his boss.

Ah, nothing like a little inappropriate workplace banter, thought Roland, who attempted a half-hearted laugh. His boss' comment hit a little too close to home. Christine seemed to be working late more often these days, and he wondered if she'd found someone else who had more of the qualities that she was looking for. He might try to be that person himself if she would ever talk to him. But he didn't know what she was thinking. He was never home either, but he wasn't stepping out behind her back. For a moment the image of Griffin smiling at him from her barstool crossed his mind.

"But really," said Perez. "Why are you spending so much time on this?"

Three other detectives sat at a table in the center of the department's open floor plan, food containers and paperwork spread out before them. One of the men was his partner, Rojas. They had been listening in on the conversation and when Roland caught Rojas' gaze, the man shook his head in disappointment.

Roland leaned back in his chair. "Why do you care? It's not costing you anything. Well, not much anyway."

"You make sure it stays that way. Honestly, I don't get it." He turned his head and called over his shoulder, "Do any of you get it?"

Rojas said, "Nope, sure don't, Captain."

Roland didn't have it in him to think up a witty comeback, so he tried honesty. "I think something is going to happen soon.

There's been more activity around the house. I've…" He hesitated before getting more honest. "I've got a hunch."

Perez leaned against the doorframe. "Oh boy. Hey fellas, Magnusson has another one of his famous hunches."

A chorus of *ooohs* came from the men at the table and Roland clenched his fists. He felt like he was back in grade school, when Garrett Holloway used to tease him about the middle-class white-bread sack lunches his mom always made him.

Perez pushed off from the door frame and came closer to Roland's desk. "You know I'm just giving you a hard time," he said in a quieter voice. "I trust your hunches. If you have a line on something, go with it. And when you need support, it'll be there."

Roland's grade-school teasing forgotten, he nodded at his boss. "Thanks."

"But that's not to say I'm gonna stop teasing you about trying to bring down a gang of little old ladies, got it?"

"Yes boss."

Perez nodded and sauntered back to his own office without another word.

Roland booted up his computer and looked up one Griffin R. Beckett of Fort Worth, Texas, and found very little. No criminal history, although her prints were on file. Also, she had no job history for the last eight years. That part puzzled him. He wanted to believe that she had told him the truth about why she was following the four ladies. In truth, he liked her. But she'd seemed stingy with the details and, until he could fill in more blanks, he knew he needed to stay vigilant.

Maybe he could find out more about her the next time he saw her. He hoped there would be a next time.

Laughter erupted outside his office and he pulled his gaze away from the computer screen to see Rojas shuffle past his door, hunched over with one arm hanging onto a cane that he must have dug up in the Lost and Found. He wasn't sure where the man had gotten the floral raincoat draped over his shoulders, but it went a long way toward creating a surprisingly realistic old-lady effect.

Rojas hobbled around the office screeching, "Eh? Eh?" and cupping one ear. "I'm gonna kick yer ass, sonny!" He waved the cane in Roland's direction.

The others laughed and someone said, "Hey Magnusson, you better arrest her for grand larceny, if you can manage it!"

Roland sighed. He wasn't in the mood. He shut down his computer, grabbed his keys off his desk, and closed the door to his office.

"Your mom wears it better," he said as he passed Rojas and left the building.

CHAPTER 13

After following the Blingsters back to their beach house from the Cheesecake Factory, Griffin sat in her rental car, hoping a Super Great Plan would magically come to her. Roland hadn't followed them, so he must have thought things were okay for the moment. But she knew that could change fast. This had to come to an end, right now, before things got out of hand. She listened to the waves for ten minutes, and no magical plan revealed itself. So she got out of the car, pulled up her pants (metaphorically speaking), and started up the stairs to the front door.

As she climbed, she heard a thumping bass line coming from inside the house. It sounded too funky to be rap and too fast to be R&B. It was also definitely not the theme song from *The Lawrence Welk Show* or *The Rockford Files*, or whatever shows oldsters liked to watch.

By the time she made it to the door, the glass panes rattled in the window frames and more of the melody was discernible. She pulled out her phone and ran the app that identifies songs. The tune was "Give Up the Funk," by Parliament. These people were serious about their funk!

Right then and there her apprehension began to turn into fear. The song screamed trouble. The Blingsters weren't to be messed with, and she needed to watch her step more carefully than she'd first thought.

She knocked on the door, but of course no one answered. Again it was unlocked, so she poked her head inside. "Hello?"

Vern and Bird Poop Man sat on one of the couches, playing Grand Theft Auto on the gigantic TV. They turned to look at her.

"She's in the kitchen!" Vern yelled over the music.

More red cups littered the coffee table now, and Griffin spotted half a reuben sandwich and some cheese puffs floating in the blue carpet as she made her way through the living room. Two women sat on the other blue floral couch, and she recognized one of them —Little Moe from the diner. Little Moe grinned a toothless smile and waved with the hand not holding a lighter. The other woman, who held a bong, didn't acknowledge Griffin. She kept her eyes closed as she blew white smoke toward the open patio door. The air smelled of peppermint, pot, and pepperoni pizza. Griffin wanted to be home so badly she thought she might cry.

G-ma stood in front of the stove, her back to Griffin, butt wiggling in time to the bass line. When she turned to the sink, Griffin saw she wore an apron and yellow latex gloves that were big enough for Shaq. She could have worn them as waders.

"Oh, hi Griffy!"

"Hi, G-ma. Are you cooking something?"

"No, just cleaning. The stove is my happy place." She smiled, old toothbrush in one hand, bottle of Super Industrial Strength Kitchen Cleaner in the other.

"Well, we're going to take you to your other happy place."

"Disneyland?" asked Marge.

"No. Come on." Griffin took the cleaning supplies from her grandmother's hands, set them on the counter, and led her to her bedroom.

"Where's your suitcase?" Griffin asked.

"I don't want to clean my suitcase!"

Was she being obtuse on purpose? "G-ma, I'm really not in the mood for this." It would have been nice if she could have told her grandma about Brian. G-ma had always been so good at taking care of her when the two spent time together in the past. She was a fantastic grandma, for sure. But now was not the time; Griffin didn't want to dump her own problems into the pot of whatever was brewing here in Florida.

"That makes two of us. Don't you have anything better to do than bother me?" Marge asked.

"No. Now where is your suitcase?"

Pause.

"Never mind, I'll find it." Griffin opened the closet. "Oh my god, this is a mess!" There were clothes and shoes and purses everywhere.

"Yes, well, I only have time to keep the stove clean. Besides, that closet is tiny! It's hard to keep anything organized in there."

Most of the clothes seemed to be jumpsuits, but about half the garments on hangers were evening dresses. Griffin marveled at how much stuff her grandma had accumulated in such a short time. Even more disconcerting was thinking about how she had afforded it all. Griffin threw a few outfits on the bed as she searched around in a pile of shoes and purses, finally finding what she was looking for.

"What on earth are you doing!" Marge said, still standing in the middle of the room wearing her giant latex gloves.

"I'm taking you back to Oklahoma. Come on, put a few things you want to take with you in there." She pointed to the suitcase. When Marge didn't move, Griffin said, "Okay, I'll do it." She picked up some of the things she'd tossed on the bed and dumped them in the open bag.

Marge let out a huff and took an armful of jumpsuits Griffin had been about to shove in the suitcase. "Fine." Marge spent a few minutes folding up the clothes and adding them to the case, along with an assortment of undergarments, shoes, and one purse. Griffin tried not to look at her grandma's lingerie, but what she saw made her blush—not even she would wear stuff that racy.

"There. Now what?" Marge glared at Griffin with her gloved hands on her hips.

Griffin walked over to her and gently took one hand and removed the glove. "Grandma, this isn't you. None of this is right. Why are you doing this?"

Griffin took off the other glove and Marge grabbed them from her and put them in the suitcase.

"I don't know what you're talking about," Marge said. "And I'll have you know this is practically kidnapping."

And here Griffin had thought maybe she could get through to her, that she could make Marge see reason. Oh well. Without saying a word, she took the jumpsuit in her grandma's hands and dropped it on the bed. Then she gave her grandma a big hug.

"Griffy! What's this about?" asked Marge.

"Nothing," said Griffin. "Nothing."

"Well I love you too, but you gotta let go of your poor G-ma or she's gonna pass out from lack of air!"

Marge laughed as Griffin moved away, and Griffin laughed too. Maybe everything would be all right. "I'm going to go get a glass of water," said Griffin. "Keep packing and I'll be right back."

"Okay!" said Marge, although Griffin knew no packing would get done while she was out of the room. At least from the kitchen she'd have a clear line of sight to the only exit out of the house, so she'd notice if her grandma tried to escape.

By now the stereo had been turned down. The Parliament song had ended and some kind of electronic music Griffin assumed was good background noise for gaming played on low. She couldn't see Vern or Big Moe from the kitchen, but she could hear them.

"Your last haul was very good, that is true," the man said.

"Are you kidding me?" said Vern. "Big Moe, you know it was better than very good. It was stellar."

Griffin was almost positive they didn't know she was right around the corner from them, so she kept quiet and stood near the cabinet where she'd found a glass the day before. If someone came into the kitchen, she'd resume her mission of getting something to drink.

"Meh," said Big Moe.

A long string of curse words left Vern's mouth.

"Aw, babe," said Little Moe in her sandpaper voice. "Cut 'em some slack." Griffin heard the bubbly noises of the bong being fired up. "This is some primo stuff," she continued, trying to hold her breath while talking.

"The next one will be better," said a voice that, if Griffin wasn't mistaken, sounded like Smitty, who must have joined her friends while Griffin was in G-ma's room.

Next *what*, Griffin wondered.

"Yes, that is what you keep saying," said Big Moe. "I hope you are correct because I have some buyers lined up and they will be very disappointed if you do not come through."

Griffin's mind raced. The Moes seemed to be an item, and it sounded like the big one was … a fence? It made sense. In order to convert their stolen stuff into cash to pay for all the crap in the house, the women needed to sell to someone. Private buyers would certainly pay better than a pawn shop, which wasn't supposed to accept stolen property. Although many of them did anyway.

"Did you talk to Marge's daughter?" Vern asked. Griffin shook her head in disgust.

Smitty corrected her. "She's her granddaughter. And yes, I made contact. She said she would see what she could do."

Griffin almost gasped. What? She thought back to running into Smitty in the diner bathroom. She'd forgotten all about interaction the until now, but clearly Smitty hadn't. It sounded like Griffin was on the verge of getting dragged into whatever was going on.

"I don't know," said Little Moe. "I don't think Big Moe is gonna like it if you guys find a replacement."

"Well, I don't think I like what you're implying," said Smitty.

"Ladies, ladies, please," said Big Moe. "While I am a firm

believer in the free market system, it is true that I would not appreciate any unwelcome competition."

Griffin started to feel faint.

"Let's just table this discussion, okay?" said Vern. "I'm sure we can figure something out that everyone can be happy with."

Except maybe for Griffin! She and G-ma had to get out and away from these people tonight.

The living room was quiet now, save for the music, the sounds from the game, and the bong gurgling away. This was Griffin's cue to get back to Marge's room.

"You don't got any water," Marge pointed out when Griffin came back.

"Huh? Oh, I drank it in the kitchen," she lied.

"I wanted some!" G-ma complained.

"No time," said Griffin. "You packed?"

"No."

"You are? Okay great, let's go." She zipped up Marge's suitcase and they closed the door behind them when they left.

"Griffin is kidnapping me," Marge announced to everyone in the living room. Now Big El was out there too.

Great, thought Griffin. That set a nice tone for their departure. She tried to laugh but it came out sounding more like she was having dental work done. "I'm not kidnapping her."

Smitty scrutinized her with a look that made Griffin feel naked.

"It's kidnapping," said Marge.

"No, it's not. We have to be back in Oklahoma tonight, that's all. She's got a dentist appointment in the morning."

"We have dentists here," said Big El.

"My cousin Lazy Moe is dentist!" said Big Moe.

There was no time to explain or argue. "Bye, y'all," Griffin said.

She managed to get Marge and her bag out the door and to the rental car, and they drove off. No one stopped them, and from what Griffin could tell, they weren't tailed when they left. That was easy!

CHAPTER 14

Marge vowed not to talk to her granddaughter for the whole drive. The absolute nerve of Griffin to waltz right into the sanctity of her own home, such as it was, and force her to leave! That house was as loud, crazy, and as messy as a crime scene on one of those CSI shows she liked to watch, but that wasn't the point. It was her choice to be there.

After a few more minutes of fuming, she realized they didn't seem to be headed to the airport. "Where are we going?" she asked, forgetting about her vow of silence.

"I have to get my things from my hotel room," said Griffin.

"Hmph," said Marge. "I paid for that room, you know."

"I know, and it was really nice."

"Then stay longer! Why don't we forget the airport and go get massages instead?"

"Nope," said Griffin.

"Hmph," said Marge.

When they arrived at the resort, Griffin made her go along to the suite while she packed up her things. Apparently Marge was not to be trusted in a vehicle by herself.

"If all your clothes look like that, dear, you should just leave them here and start over back home." Marge pointed to a cardigan sweater laid out on the bed. The girl was cute but dressed like an accountant. Oh wait, wasn't Griffy an accountant, or something like that? In which case, the clothes made sense, but still. No zazz.

Griffin glared at her but said nothing as she zipped up her suitcase. She took one more look around the room, and ushered Marge back out again, all in less than five minutes.

They were back on the freeway and Griffin asked, "Why did you guys go to the Cheesecake Factory?"

"Why not?" said Marge. What a dumb question! Everyone knew they had the best fried appetizers. Griffin looked confused, so she continued. "They have great senior specials. And my canasta team can spread out in their private room. More space to practice." Then it hit her. "Hey, wait a minute! How did you know where we were?"

Griffin was silent.

Marge started to fume even more and said nothing until they passed a sign on the freeway for the Miami International Airport.

"This is not cool," she said.

"Nothing about this trip is cool," agreed Griffin.

Marge tried another angle. "What about Otto?"

"I'll take care of him tomorrow."

"You have all the answers, don't you young lady," snapped Marge. Griffin said nothing. "What you and your parents are doing is criminal! I'm an adult. I can make decisions for myself!"

"Like the time last Easter when you and Gertrude stole that security guard's golf cart and drove it into the pool in your apartment complex?"

Marge laughed. "Yeah, that was pretty funny!" Then she realized she'd just helped Griffin's case. "But that was different."

"Oh yeah? How's that?"

"That was kid stuff. Immature pranks. The Blingsters got real sophistication! They're real swanky-like. I've never known anyone like them before. And they like me!"

"Look," said Griffin as she got off the freeway. "I get it, honest. But I don't think they're good people."

"Griffy, no offense, but I don't trust your judgment. I love you whole bunches, but even you have to admit you're not much of a people person. So let your ol' G-ma have this one, okay? I've been around the block a few times."

Griffin said nothing and her eyes never left the road. Marge sighed. Perhaps she had gone too far. But she was tired of having her motives questioned at every turn. It had been happening for a while; like a person hit a certain age and all of a sudden their family thought they were losing it. Just because someone drove a golf cart into a pool didn't mean they were infirm. More likely it meant they were bored. And that was how the whole cruise thing had started in the first place. She'd asked Gertrude to go with her, but her friend had declined, citing varicose vein problems. Marge decided to go on her own and while it was scary at first, she was glad she did it. Now she had new friends and a chance at a new life. So phooey on Griffy and Riffy!

"Mom and Dad would kill me if something happened to you, G-ma. We need to get you home."

"This is ridiculous! It's not fair! I am not incapable or feeble, I'm a young thing. And I'm in great shape, other than a bit of bursitis in my left elbow."

"G-ma, why is all of this happening?" Griffin asked. "Why can't you be happy with your old life? Can't you go back to how things used to be?"

"You don't understand," said Marge. No one in her family seemed to. "None of that feels good enough anymore. None of it has any *life* in it."

"The last thing I want to do is restrict how you live. But this? This is dangerous here, G-ma! It's for the best, really."

"Hmph." Marge didn't know what else to say. Clearly they thought she couldn't take care of herself. Had they always thought that? She'd been on her own for the last twenty years after divorcing that loser husband of hers. And she'd been doing things her way for much longer than twenty years—taking care of everyone, working, making ends meet. They never noticed before; why did they care now? Her own granddaughter had tailed her to a Cheesecake Factory for heaven's sake!

Well, thought Marge, she would show them. The girl wanted to tail her? Game on.

Less than half an hour later, they'd dropped off the rental car, taken the shuttle bus to the terminal, and were standing in line to buy two last-minute tickets out of town. Marge couldn't seem to get a minute alone so she could try to contact her fellow Blingsters. Griffin hadn't even let her go to the restroom by herself.

"These tickets are going to cost a fortune," said Griffin.

"So what?" said Marge. "That husband of yours is loaded."

"No, he's not," she said sharply as she dug around in her purse, which looked like it had way too many pockets and compartments.

"What?" asked Marge, surprised. She looked at Griffin's face now, and what she saw there concerned her. Her granddaughter looked like she might cry. "Is everything all right?"

"It's a long story. I'll tell you when we're on the plane."

"Okay Griffy." She patted Griffin's arm.

There were two people ahead of them in line. Marge's time was running out. "I'm thirsty. Can I go get a root beer? I'll leave you my credit card for the tickets." That wasn't an ideal situation, but it was the best she could think up.

"No."

One person ahead of them in line. Think, think, think. She loved her granddaughter, and something seemed to be bothering her. She didn't want to abandon her now, but at the same time, Griffin was an adult and would be able to navigate the situation on her own. Marge promised herself she'd bake cookies for her favorite granddaughter when this was all over. Whenever that was. Right now, bigger things were at stake, like her independence.

She tried again. "I don't feel so good."

"We can sit down in a minute," said Griffin.

It was their turn to buy tickets.

Griffin walked up to the ticket counter and Marge followed with zero enthusiasm. She stood right behind her granddaughter, who hefted first her own suitcase onto the stainless-steel scale, then Marge's.

"And where will you be flying today?" said the ticket agent, a pleasant-looking woman, probably in her sixties. She smiled at Griffin, who didn't seem to notice, so her eye moved to Marge, who smiled back.

"We'd like two one-way tickets to Oklahoma City please," said Griffin, searching through her purse again.

Marge seized her opportunity. She would miss her favorite jumpsuits that she'd packed in the suitcase, but it was a small price to pay for freedom. She caught the agent's gaze again, and after giving the woman her best smile, held an index finger to her lips. The agent nodded once, and Marge was gone.

CHAPTER 15

Griffin's sweet little grandma had given her the slip at the Miami International Airport. She was never going to hear the end of it when they all got together for Thanksgiving. Especially if Marge hadn't resurfaced by then.

The ticket agent claimed ignorance, insisting that she'd been typing on her screen and hadn't seen what happened. One minute Marge was there, the next she'd vanished into thin air. Yeah, right.

She needed to collect her thoughts, so she sat down on a bench across from the ticket counter. Her emotions bounced all over the place, from anger to fear to frustration, making a brief stop in overwhelm, careening back to fear, and then landing squarely in overwhelm again.

What should she do next? She could guess where to find her G-ma, that wasn't the problem. The problem was what to do once she found her. Those Blingsters were more than a little bit scary! And even if she could outmaneuver them, her grandma wasn't being very cooperative. The woman had given her the slip once already, and if hard pressed, might prove to be more slippery than a buttered eel.

Assuming Griffin could "catch" her grandma, what then? Maybe she could physically force Marge to get on a plane with her, but how would she explain that to TSA? The woman would surely make a scene; no telling what she might accuse Griffin of in public. Nope, she would have to use logic or maybe some other form of coercion besides physical force. She didn't think she was up for the task.

This was supposed to have been a quick trip to Florida to bring G-ma home. But now she was in way over her head.

Griffin took deep breaths. There had to be something she could do. Then she had an idea. Yes, there was only one thing to be done.

But first, she would have to spend more money to rent another car. And before that she needed food, or she was going to fall down from low blood sugar. The one beer she'd consumed at the Cheesecake Factory wasn't helping. She was by no means intoxicated, just extra hungry. Usually she didn't drink, but she hadn't wanted the cop to think she was a nerd (although she totally was). Regardless, she needed something to eat.

The only two things in the part of the airport she could get to without a ticket were a grilled cheese food truck parked in front of the TSA entrance—how did they get a truck inside the airport? She couldn't even bring in a bottle of water—and some dive called Flammo's Coffee and Crab Shack, which looked more than a little sketchy.

In hindsight, an overpriced grilled three-cheese sandwich, while delicious, might not have been the best snack choice. It certainly made waiting in line at the Super Cheapo Mega Budget Car Rental Company counter more interesting as she juggled a gooey sandwich, a handful of greasy napkins, and her purse and suitcase. When she finally got to an available agent, she placed the container holding her half-eaten food on the counter and started digging through her purse for her wallet.

"I need a car," she said, still digging.

"For how long?" asked the rental agent, who watched her with detached amusement. The man probably saw all sorts of tourist chaos coming through his line.

Griffin stopped digging and looked at him. "I have no idea," she said.

"I can't rent you a car for an undetermined period of time." He gave Griffin a look that suggested he was sorry for her lack of intelligence, and he would do the best he could with what god had given her.

"Fine. One week." She hoped with all her heart that she would not still be in Florida in one week, but it seemed better to overshoot than not keeping the car for long enough.

The man began typing on his terminal and Griffin continued the search for her wallet. She vowed to buy a new bag as soon as possible—one that had fewer pockets. Better yet, no pockets.

"Would you like to be able to bring the car back with an empty tank?" he asked.

"Okay."

"And which level of insurance would you like?" He flashed her a laminated card that described three levels of rental insurance.

"Basic."

The agent looked smug as he typed some more.

"Aha!" Griffin said and held up her billfold. Then she searched through the wallet, which also had too many pockets, until she found her credit card.

"Please sign," said the man.

Griffin pushed a couple prompts on the signature pad, signed her acceptance of all the terms of the rental, and stuck her card in the card reader. She and the agent waited. Nothing happened.

"Let me see that," said the agent. He turned the reader on its swivel base so he could read the screen but pulled his hand away and grimaced. "What did you get all over this thing?" he asked, finding a paper towel under the counter to wipe off his hands with.

"What? Oh sorry, I guess that's grease from my sandwich."

"Yes, well." He made another face as he tried to wipe the little screen off.

"Grilled cheese. So good."

"Uh-huh."

When the screen was clean, he hit a few more buttons and they waited again. Nothing happened.

Something bing-bonged on his computer. "It says your card is declined."

"No," said Griffin, incredulous.

"Yes," said the man, mocking incredulity.

That couldn't be! She paid the card off in full every month. It was her and Brian's joint card... What if Brian had closed the account or worse yet, maxed the card out and left the balance for her to pay off. That little shit!

"Okay," said Griffin, trying to slow her breathing down. She couldn't afford to panic. She couldn't afford much of anything at the moment, and panic would have to wait. She'd used almost all her cash to pay for her overpriced airport sandwich. No credit card, not much cash. Oy. She started to panic again.

"Okay?" the agent asked, raising an eyebrow.

Oh yeah, payment. "Um..." She fished around in her wallet and in a secret pocket found her emergency money—a Visa gift card with $500 on it. "If I bring the car back early, can I get a refund?"

"No," he said, with far less politeness than before.

"Okay, in that case I will rent the cheapest car you have for three days."

Again the agent made a sour face and began redoing all the contracts. As she waited, Griffin picked up the laminated card with the insurance information on it. "Hey!" she said. "All this insurance is optional!"

"Yes," said the agent in a bored tone.

"You made it sound like I needed some!"

"I simply asked you which package you wanted."

They argued for a few minutes, Griffin accusing him of upselling her without her approval while he accused her of getting his workstation all greasy. But he did capitulate and remove the optional insurance, costing Griffin another ten minutes as he redid all the paperwork for a third time, but it saved her enough money to be able to extend the rental by one day.

"This is going in my Yelp review," she snapped as he handed her the keys and receipt.

"Okay," he said. "Have a nice day."

CHAPTER 16

The sandwich had gone cold by the time Griffin got into her rental car—a tiny Chevy Spark that made her feel claustrophobic. All she could think of as she pulled out of the lot was that two decent-sized SUVs would be able to play hockey with her Spark and she'd be helpless.

She ate the rest of the grilled cheese while trying to exit the airport and when it was gone (most in her belly, some in her pile of napkins on the passenger seat, a little more on her pants), she connected her phone to the car's Bluetooth. Time to call in the big guns. She was in over her head and needed help. She hated to do it but knew she wouldn't be able to handle the Blingsters on her own, and she also wasn't sure Roland would be the most understanding person. There was no way around it, she needed to make this call.

"Hello? Griffin?"

"Hi Grandma Delphine, it's Griffin."

"I got that part, dear. How are you? What's going on? It sounds like you're driving."

"Yeah, I am. Listen, I'm not bothering you right now, am I?"

"No, not at all. I was just having a bite to eat before leaving for my ballroom dancing club. Grilled cheese, my favorite!"

"How do you know what I'm eating?" said Griffin.

"What?" said Delphine.

"Wait, what?"

"Griffin, I'm glad you called, really I am. But could you get to the point? I've got less than half my life left."

"Sorry," Griffin said, distracted by a semi that had part of an airplane fuselage strapped to its trailer. She could see the seats inside and everything—it was like someone had chopped the front half of a plane off and decided to take it for a spin down the freeway. The airline's logo was still visible on the side. The whole thing didn't instill much confidence in the company, but she'd never enjoyed flying much to begin with. "I think G-ma is in trouble."

"Oh? What has Marge gone and done this time?"

"I'm not exactly sure," Griffin said as she cut across a lane of traffic to get on a different freeway. Those kinds of driving indiscretions never counted against you when you were traveling in an unfamiliar city, right?

"That's a good start, but not a lot to go on."

It all seemed so ridiculous that Griffin hesitated to say anything out loud. But unless Marge was playing some spectacular prank on everyone, it was really happening.

"We're in Florida," Griffin continued. "Long story about how she got here, we can save that for another day. Mom and Dad made me come out here to take her back to Oklahoma, but she ditched me at the airport an hour ago."

"And? Surely you can handle that. Didn't you get training?"

"Not that kind of training," said Griffin in a meek voice. She'd barely passed the required coursework and only got hired by the Bureau because of her knowledge of securities, not her knowledge of people.

"Mmm." Delphine sounded disappointed.

Griffin paused, still debating whether to put it all out there.

What the heck.

"I think she might be in deep with some jewel thieves." And

that was the moment Griffin remembered the giant diamond. Her giant diamond. Maybe it was a good thing she hadn't tried to get on a plane—what would that thing have looked like on the TSA X-ray monitor? How would she ever have explained it?

And then Griffin remembered that she'd forgotten to put the diamond in her luggage. It was still in the safe in her room at the resort.

Through all the freaking out, Griffin had started to drift into another lane and was jolted back to the present moment by a long-haired guy in a Subaru Outback who honked and gave her the finger as he passed by.

"Griffin?"

"I'm okay!"

"What?"

"Wait, what?"

Delphine must have asked her something, but she hadn't heard it. She was lucky to still be on the road.

"I said, what did your mother say about it?"

Griffin had dropped the ball on that too—she'd been so busy she'd forgotten to update her parents. Not that they had called her either, but maybe that was because they were expecting her to be bringing her grandma back that night.

"Well?" Delphine asked.

"Um, so, like, I didn't tell them."

Four seconds of silence that could only be described as disapproving followed.

"But I will, I swear! I'll call them as soon as I get back to … to wherever I'm going." Another thing to work out. She wanted to start looking for her G-ma, but would Marge be so transparent as to head right back to her beach house? If she didn't go there, where *would* she go?

Maybe Griffin should go back to the resort and check on the diamond first. If someone thought she'd checked out and started cleaning the room and happened to check the safe…

Griffin was close to panicking. Which got her another honk,

this time from a late-model GMC pickup truck with custom lift suspension and a gun rack in the back window.

"You really shouldn't talk while you drive, dear. Now let me get this straight. Marge is involved with thieves? Hmm. Now why doesn't that surprise me," Delphine said the words in a totally unsurprised-sounding voice.

"I don't know. Why *doesn't* that surprise you?" As far as Griffin was aware, her two grandmas didn't know each other very well. But maybe she had been mistaken there too. Anything was possible at this point.

Delphine was silent for a few more seconds. "Okay. Where are you staying? I'll be there in a few hours."

"How is that possible?" Griffin asked. "You can't get here that fast from LA."

Delphine sighed. "I'm in Virginia. I can catch the next flight out from Reagan National."

"Oh, okay," said Griffin, trying to follow along. She knew if she asked about the fib, she wouldn't get a straight answer, so she dropped it.

"Are you going to tell me where you're staying?" asked Delphine.

In theory, Griffin had checked out of the resort. But had she? She couldn't remember if she'd left the key card behind or not. Regardless, she needed to try to get back in to recover the gemstone. "Let me get back to you on that."

"You don't have a place to stay?"

"I think I do?"

"Well don't ask me, dear. *I* don't know."

"I'll text you the address later," said Griffin.

"I can hardly wait," said Delphine.

CHAPTER 17

Delphine ended the call with her granddaughter and stood in the middle of a hallway of a seven-story, nondescript concrete building in Arlington, Virginia. She tapped her phone with her index finger, collecting her thoughts. She had flown to the East Coast from Los Angeles with her former colleague, Kenji Yamamoto, at the request of the current director of the top-secret organization they both used to work for. She'd done it as a favor to her former boss, Richard Dere. Both she and Kenji were retired, but it was the kind of job that one never fully retired from.

At this point in her life, she tried to be sure that family came first, but it hadn't always been that way. Because her work schedule had always been both busier and more secretive than most people's, she'd never attended many family functions in Oklahoma and hadn't gotten to know Marge Flanders very well. But she liked Griffin exceedingly well, and if her granddaughter needed help, she would oblige. First however, she needed to find a way to excuse herself from the meeting in the conference room down the hall.

"What's up?" said a familiar voice behind her. Her old partner Kenji Yamamoto stood there, inspecting her face for information.

She was good at hiding emotions, but he was better at figuring her out. "Oh. Trouble," he said.

"A little family issue," said Delphine. "I need to get to Florida tonight. Can you help me out here?"

He nodded, and a mischievous sparkle flashed in his eyes.

Just like the good old days.

"Thank you." She smoothed out the front of her blazer. "Okay, let's go."

They went back into the conference room and took their seats at the shiny mahogany table, where twenty people sat waiting for them. Only one person was a woman, the rest were white males over the age of fifty-five. Once again Delphine sent up a prayer that the established hierarchy would eventually change.

"Mrs. Lougheed, why don't you continue?" said the suit at the head of the table.

"Certainly, Director Smith. Now where were we? Oh yes, Legos."

The director looked alarmed. The rest of the attendees appeared confused.

Kenji leaned toward Delphine and said, "You mean Mid-East operations."

"What? Oh! Yes, the Mid-East. Right. Well, I believe that the demographics for Duplo sets are younger than our primary targets, and…" Delphine's voice trailed off. She plonked her elbows on the table and put her head in her hands.

The director leaned forward in his seat. Everyone else leaned back.

"Is she okay?" asked Director Smith.

Kenji wheeled his chair closer to his friend and placed a hand on her shoulder. "Delphine?"

"Whose birthday are we celebrating?" she mumbled.

"I'm sorry," said Kenji, looking at the director. "I think she is unwell. It started this morning, but I thought she had enough energy for the meeting. Apparently not. She has good days and bad days, you know."

The director nodded but said nothing, and Delphine looked up at the ceiling. "The lights!"

Kenji stood up and gently pulled Delphine out of her chair and led her toward the door. "I'd better get her back to the hotel."

"Of course," said the director. "But what about the report?"

Delphine and Kenji didn't hear his question, as they were already twenty feet down the hall. Kenji let go of her arm when they got to the elevator.

"That was a snoozefest," said Delphine. "I figured you probably wanted out too."

"Thank you, very thoughtful," said Kenji. "It was indeed a total snoozefest. I don't know why they still make us do these things. Technically, we aren't employed anymore."

"I think the nature of our work and who we do it for means we're always employed, whether we want to be or not."

"Mmm," said Kenji.

They left the building and headed down the street toward their hotel, which was within walking distance of the Pentagon.

"Will you go back to LA?" she asked.

Kenji sighed as he thought about the question. "Oh, I might go to the National Gallery first, but yes, I will go home tomorrow. Want me to pick up your mail?"

"That would be nice. I'm not sure when I'll be back. My son-in-law's mother seems to have gotten into a spot of trouble, and I don't know how long it'll take me to clean it up." Delphine and Kenji lived across the street from each other. She'd moved to Pasadena first, after her husband died, and he'd followed not long after. The two of them had been partners, and at one time more than that, but now they were the best of friends and watched over each other's houses when one of them went away.

"Do you want me to come with you?" Kenji asked.

"That's awfully nice of you, but no, I think I can take care of it. You go home and relax. I'll call you if I change my mind."

When they got to their hotel, they said goodbye in the lobby. Delphine went to her room, and Kenji left again, heading to the

Metro station to go into DC. She packed her small case of things and checked flights out of Reagan National. Two more flights to Miami that night. Piece of cake.

She just hoped she wasn't walking into a situation that was the complete opposite of a piece of cake.

CHAPTER 18

After hanging up with Delphine, Griffin pulled off the freeway and spent ten minutes looking through all the pockets in her purse, confirming that she'd forgotten to leave the key card to her hotel suite behind and still had it with her. Thank goodness!

She headed back to the resort. Everything would be fine; the hotel didn't know she had intended to leave. The reservation G-ma had made for her was good for one more day, and with Delphine's help, maybe they could extend their stay.

She realized it might seem strange to someone outside the family to discover that she had called one grandma to help her get the other one out of trouble. But if she were going to call anyone for help, Delphine would be the person.

Griffin's mom Greta Beckett was Delphine Lougheed's daughter. Greta was married to Riff Flanders, G-ma's son and Griffin's dad. Griffin had no idea why almost everyone in her family had different last names from each other—she'd asked Delphine about it several times, but never got a straight answer.

Griffin grew up calling her grandma by her first name instead of Granny or Memaw or whatever, because she wasn't the cute nickname kind of grandma. Delphine had always been a mysterious figure, especially when Griffin was a kid. Griffin had never been able to spend much time with Delphine, because her grandma lived far away in exotic Pasadena, California. And when everyone got together for holidays or other celebrations, it was difficult to coordinate Delphine's presence because of how much traveling she did for work. As a result, Griffin didn't know much about her.

No one seemed to know what Delphine's "work" entailed. Perhaps Griffin's parents knew, but they never shared it with her. She tried to ask them, but they were always evasive, like Delphine.

A few years earlier, Griffin managed to piece together a theory that Delphine was employed by a government agency. Or maybe it was an international agency? Griffin couldn't find out its name or purpose, even with her own security clearance. And it was impossible to determine whether Delphine was retired or not. But she was in her seventies, like G-ma, for heaven's sake, so she must have been!

What Griffin did know for sure was that Delphine was a badass. She was smart, sassy, knew about different cultures all over the world, and one Christmas Eve, after overdoing the eggnog, she let it slip that she knew how to kill a man with nothing but a hairpin.

That was why when Delphine had originally told Griffin she was about to go ballroom dancing in Pasadena but then changed her story to admit she was in Virginia, Griffin hadn't thought too much about it. It was par for the course in her grandmother's line of work. Whatever it was.

That was also why as soon as G-ma had given her the slip, Griffin knew she needed to call Delphine. She only hoped it wasn't too late.

Griffin made it back to her room and collapsed on the bed, exhausted and worried and a little embarrassed at how far off her game she was. She had lost her own grandma!

In her mind she saw the growing list of her failures: she was holding onto a large diamond that had a questionable origin story at best. She had made her beloved G-ma mad and thought that another man besides her husband was cute. She'd also forgotten said large diamond in the hotel safe when supposedly checking out of her room, then lost one grandmother and had to call the other one for help. Wait. The diamond!

Griffin sprang from the bed and went to the safe, sighing with relief after she opened it and found her sport socks, still with a giant lump in them. Just to be sure everything was okay, she took the diamond out of the socks and held it in her hand.

It was stunning. She'd never seen anything like it! But was that a good enough reason for pocketing it? She still couldn't explain that one. It had all happened so fast, like she had acted on instinct. But what kind of instinct?

And what to do about it? The right thing probably would have been to give it to Rolly, but at this point she didn't think she could do that without it looking stupendously bad. Especially with no FBI connections to provide her some semblance of propriety.

But instead of thinking it all through, she put the diamond back in the socks and into the safe, and proceeded to do what most people did when forced to face their future: pretend it didn't exist.

Next, she texted Delphine with the information for the resort and her room number. After changing out of her cheese-laden clothes and into something clean, she tried to watch some TV, but it was all such garbage. Didn't anyone make shows meant for people with more than two brain cells? She flipped back and forth between a sitcom (sadly, not animated) about dog lawyers who represented people and a show (sadly, not a sitcom) about a real-life rap star named P-Taco who had recently discovered Buddhism. She turned the set off after a few minutes.

Griffin wanted to feel useful. Maybe she should go by G-ma's bachelorette pad before Delphine arrived and check up on the Blingsters. Maybe they were having another party … Or perhaps they were out. Who knew what kind of trouble they might be getting into if they were out somewhere though. Her head hurt just thinking about it. But she could at least go and do some recon while she waited for the big grandma guns to arrive.

Griffin got her purse and rummaged around in all the little hidey-hole pocket thingies. She was looking for loose change, but all she came up with was a business card … for one Detective Roland Magnusson. What a smarty pants! He must have thought he was so clever, sneaking it into her purse at the Cheesecake Factory. Actually, that had been pretty clever.

Rolly picked up on the second ring. "Magnusson," he said in a quiet, police detective-y voice. He sounded so smooth Griffin forgot what she'd been planning to say.

"Shrimp," she blurted, then slapped her hand to her forehead.

Roland was silent, perhaps wondering if he'd gotten a strange spam call.

"Hi, Rolly."

"Oh, it's you."

"You sound like every other man in my life," she muttered.

"Excuse me?"

"What's new? Out on a date?"

"No, I'm working."

"Where?"

"I can't say." At that point, Roland must have fumbled the phone because what followed was a muffled "Dammit!" and the sound of the phone's mic rustling against some fabric. He didn't seem to be the most coordinated person. "Where are you?" he asked when he'd regained control of the situation. "You better be back in Texas."

"Oh sure. I'm nowhere near Florida. Just called to say hi."

"Okay, hi."

"So what are you doing?" Griffin tried again.

"I'm going door-to-door asking people if they've seen a lost kitten."

"Really? Where?"

"No, not really. And I'm not going to tell you where I am," he said.

"Oh."

She'd thought maybe she could come up with an elaborate ruse to find out where he was, but anything more complicated than basic questioning seemed to be out of her wheelhouse.

There was a pause and then Roland spoke with some hesitancy in his voice. "You know, I'm in Dallas sometimes for work. Conferences and such. Maybe I'll look you up next time I'm there. We could … well…"

Griffin pinched the bridge of her nose. Great. Her attempt to find out his location seemed to have given him the wrong idea. An unintended consequence. Maybe.

"See you later, Rolly," she said and hung up, not realizing till several seconds later that her sign-off could be interpreted several different ways.

What an unproductive phone call. All she'd wanted was to find out whether Detective Magnusson was anywhere near the beach house, but no dice. Now she was a little depressed for some reason.

She could continue to sit around and wait for Delphine, or she could take matters into her own hands. That sounded more interesting.

CHAPTER 19

Griffin pulled up to the curb about ten houses down from the Blingsters' party pad, figuring that if Rolly was around, he'd probably have parked closer than that. There was no sign of his car anywhere, though, including down the street in the other direction, past the house. Good.

The house looked empty as she approached it, or quiet at least. G-ma's Benz was in the carport, but no other cars were around and the porch light was off. Griffin crept up the stairs and, using some skills she *did* happen to remember from her training, let herself into the house.

No one was home, and she reasoned it was probably okay if she looked around a little, since she happened to be in the neighborhood. She turned on a lamp sitting on a side table, casting a dim light through the living room and a few yards down the hallway. Visibility was good enough to do a little snooping, so she waded through the living room carpet, unable to miss the fact that the place was even dirtier than it had been before. And she had just been there a few hours earlier. It already seemed like a lifetime ago.

Now as she stood there, she was apprehensive of what she might find and unsure of where she should start looking. She also wasn't sure what she wanted to find in the first place. But what she discovered made her stomach drop.

Strewn on the dinette table in front of the sliding glass door was a collection of interesting items. There was a box of bullets, only half full. Next to that lay some kind of hunting knife and a few black velvet pouches, the kind you might see in those old movies about big jewelry heists. The thieves would pull one of those pouches out of their coat pocket and pour a brilliant cache of diamonds into someone's palm. Griffin checked each bag. Empty.

What did the items mean? The tableau could represent any number of things. The hunting knife might be for cutting up a rotisserie chicken for dinner, the pouches were for storing expensive hearing aids, and the bullets might be headed for the Goodwill giveaway box.

A second possible scenario was that the Blingsters had, at the last minute, changed their minds about participating in some kind of criminal activity and left everything behind to drive to the casino, like every other self-respecting Florida senior.

Or these were their leftover supplies for a "job" of some sort. But if the deadly-looking hunting knife was an extra item, she would hate to see what knife had made the cut. So to speak.

Her heart couldn't decide if it wanted to leap into her throat or drop into her stomach. Either way, Griffin had a bad feeling about what might be happening elsewhere in Florida at that moment.

She was about to look around the apartment more, but her phone buzzed in her back pocket. When she pulled it out, there was Grandma Lougheed's picture on the screen.

"Hello?" whispered Griffin.

"I'm downstairs," said Delphine.

"Okay," said Griffin. "I left a keycard for you at the front desk, didn't you get my text? Anyway, feel free to go on up to the room and make yourself comfortable. I'm out right now … picking up a pizza."

"Well that's nice, but I'm downstairs at the beach house you just broke into."

"Hold on a sec." Griffin crept to the front door, opened it a crack, and peered down the stairs. Sure enough, there was Delphine looking up at her. She gave Griffin an exasperated look and pointedly tapped on her phone's screen to end the call.

She came up the steps and into the house, and Griffin closed the door behind them.

"How did you do that?" Griffin asked.

"Which part?" Delphine said.

"All of it! How did you get here so fast? How did you know where I was?"

"Griffin, there are some things about your grandma that should probably remain a mystery to you. Now, what have you found?"

"Bullets, a knife, and gemstone pouches." Griffin pointed to the table.

"I see."

"You do?"

Delphine didn't say anything, instead heading for the back of the house. She went down the hall and silently opened each door, stuck her head in to look around, and closed it again. Her last stop was the kitchen, where she observed the tower of pizza boxes before joining Griffin back at the dinette table.

"This place is a disgusting mess," Delphine said in a calm voice. "Did they have a party?"

"G-ma says it's like this all the time," said Griffin.

"I don't know what she's into, but she's definitely in it."

They stood at the table, Griffin not wanting to say anything in case Delphine was deep in thought and about to blow the whole thing wide open.

Delphine picked up the box of bullets. "Nine millimeter."

"Is that significant?" Griffin asked.

"Probably not to you."

At that moment, they heard a car door shut outside and not

too far away. Delphine clutched her purse to her side and crept to the window to look out onto the street. Griffin went to join her but got reprimanded.

"Stay back!" Delphine hissed, and tried to push her granddaughter away.

"Oh pish," said Griffin, and stood next to her at the window.

"He looks dangerous," Delphine whispered.

They watched as Detective Magnusson walked from his unmarked car, parked a few houses down the street, and disappeared from their view. He was under the house, probably looking at G-ma's Benz.

"Nah, that's only Rolly." As soon as Griffin said it, she realized what his presence implied. He'd wring their necks for being in the house. "Uh-oh."

They stood by the window and waited for another glimpse of Roland, but none was forthcoming. Then they heard footsteps on the stairs. Quiet but firm, just like him.

"Fudgsicles," Griffin said.

"Police?" Delphine asked.

"Yeah. We're gonna get so busted!"

"Not if I can help it." Delphine gave Griffin a light shove and pointed to the hallway. Griffin considered hiding in Big El's room, since it was closest, but didn't want to get tangled in a trapeze or fall into some other weird setup. Instead, she kept walking and led them into G-ma's room, where Delphine wordlessly instructed her to get in the closet.

"This is the best you could come up with?" whispered Griffin as she started to pull the sliding door closed. She tried to look around to find a good place to stand, but she couldn't see a thing and there didn't seem to be much space. She lost her balance and ended up falling onto Delphine's lap.

"Excuse you!" whispered Delphine.

"Sorry," said Griffin, who managed to ease her way into a space that must have been created by the recently liberated suitcase. Hopefully whatever Delphine might be sitting on wasn't too pointy or uncomfortable. Griffin reached for the sliding door to close it the rest of the way, but some clothing blocked the track.

"We're lucky some of her things are gone, otherwise we'd be hiding under the bed."

"There's probably stuff under there too. How can one woman buy so much?" whispered Delphine. "She hasn't been living here that long, has she?"

"No, I think she just likes to shop."

They sat there for a few moments, listening, but Griffin didn't hear any noise from the front of the house.

"Now what?" asked Griffin. "Do we wait for him to find us here and beg for forgiveness for trespassing?"

"Shush. He's not supposed to come in here either, don't forget. This is a precaution."

It was very dark in the closet, but Griffin heard Delphine unzip her purse with a steady hand. As her eyes adjusted to the dark, she thought she saw her grandma pull out a small pistol and just about fainted. "You can't *shoot* him!"

"Did you ever ask to see his ID?" Delphine countered.

"He gave me a business card…"

Delphine let out a sigh. "Oh, Griffin. Such an amateur move."

Now that both of her grandmothers had each proclaimed her an amateur, Griffin decided it was definitely time to reevaluate her life choices. Or find a good therapist. Maybe both. But Delphine was right. She couldn't say with 100% certainty that Roland was a real detective. Or even that his name was Roland.

CHAPTER 20

Detective Roland Magnusson sat in his unmarked car, parked on the darkened street three houses down from the ladies' beach house, windows down to enjoy the cool ocean breeze.

On a whim, he'd left the police station after finishing his paperwork and instead of returning home to an empty apartment, drove back to the beach house. Christina was at the lanes with her bowling league tonight, or so she'd told him. She knew he hated bowling, and now he wondered if she was lying to him with the perfect cover, knowing he'd never look for her at a bowling alley. Regardless, she wasn't home, and he wasn't in the mood to do laundry. And the longer he sat in his car watching the house, the more he had the feeling that tonight would be the night.

Now he had one eye watching out for his sketchy senior suspects and the other on the vegan tofu tacos on a paper plate in his lap. They were surprisingly good. Maybe he'd consider going vegan. Anything was possible.

He'd been surveilling the house for a while, but the four women were gone when he got there and hadn't come back yet. Eventually he became so hungry that he left in search of food. The closest thing he could find was a taco truck in a Super Target parking lot that served nothing but vegan food. Then, after a quick stop to gas up his car and buy a bag full of snacks from the convenience store (stress eating in his line of work was a real thing), he sped back to the house and took up his position again. Just as he was about to tuck into his second taco, he realized that something was off—now there was a light on upstairs.

He put the tacos aside, got out of his car, and walked up the wooden stairs to the front door, which he knocked on a few times. No answer.

However, the door was not locked.

Perhaps the ladies always left their door unlocked. Having no explicit invitation to enter the premises, he knew he should turn around and leave.

Or he could take the unlocked door as a sign of possible foul play, and enter the house out of concern for someone who might be in trouble inside.

He went in and closed the door behind him.

It was very quiet in the house, and the weak light from one reading lamp on a side table illuminated a scene that reminded him of his college days. No, it was worse than his college days. Maybe he'd been right to enter the house; he began to think he might find someone in distress in the midst of the mess.

He walked into the living room and stopped short of two couches the size of cruise ships to listen. It sounded like there was whispered arguing coming from down the hallway. He removed his gun from its holster and held it in one hand, gripped his small flashlight in the other, and crossed his wrists. Then he began to creep down the hall, lighting the way for himself and his weapon.

It was moments like this that he felt like a parody of himself. He called them 'Hawaii 5-O' moments. They felt fake, set up for entertainment. Something you would see in a cheesy TV show. But no, he really was creeping down the hall of a senior-citizen sorority house.

The whispering grew louder, and when he got to the second door on his left, he crept into the room. Now he could tell the voices were coming from the closet. One side of the double sliding doors was slightly open, and when his light flashed along the gap, the whispering stopped. Keeping the light shining at the floor, he strode up to the closet and in one swift movement slid the door open.

His gun was pointed at two women sitting on a pile of clothes and shoes and purses. And one of the women was pointing a gun right back at him.

"You need to drop that right now," he said in a firm voice.

The woman with the gun, whom he now noticed looked like she was in her seventies, said, "You should follow your own suggestion."

"It's not a suggestion! Drop it!"

The woman didn't move.

"It's okay, Grandma, he's fine. Look, he has a badge," the other woman said.

"Could be fake," said the grandma.

Roland stole a quick glance at the other woman. "Griffin?"

"Hi Rolly."

"I told you not to call me that. Who is this woman?"

"Who are *you*?" asked Delphine.

Griffin started to stand up, but then said, "Ow!" and fell back into the closet.

"What is it? Are you okay?" he asked.

"My back cramped up from sitting on that pile of purses," she said.

Roland held out a hand to help her up, and she accepted. But as soon as she was standing, he pointed his gun at Delphine again and they recommenced their staring contest.

"This is stupid," said Griffin. "Delphine, meet Roland. Roland, meet Delphine."

Delphine looked at Griffin, who nodded, and she finally lowered her gun. Roland lowered his.

"I'll need to see some ID," they both said in unison. Griffin laughed at them.

A few minutes later they had all inspected each other's IDs

and were seated at the dinette table. Griffin's license he'd seen before, so that was fine, but this Delphine Lougheed person seemed a little fishy. Her driver's license was from California, so right off the bat he knew she was one of those West-Coast weirdos. He would have loved to run her ID through the computer, but that meant having to dig his laptop out from his trunk. If she was with Griffin, maybe she was all right herself. But he couldn't be certain.

They sat looking at the items on the table—the half-empty box of bullets, the very sharp knife, and the velvet gem pouches. Griffin's hands were placed face-down on the tabletop, per Roland's instructions, as were Delphine's. When Delphine had expressed disdain for the directive, he explained that it was either that or handcuffs. She'd complied but kept giving him angry looks across the table.

"So now what?" asked Griffin.

"What were you doing in the closet?" Roland asked.

"What were you doing inside the house?" asked Delphine.

Roland pointed at Delphine. "You, quiet." He looked at Griffin. "What are you doing here?"

Delphine raised her hand as if asking permission to speak, which only made Roland crankier. The only thing he hated worse than a smart-ass was … Nope, there was nothing he hated more than a smart-ass.

"We were—" Griffin had started to speak but Delphine cut her off.

"We are visiting Marge Flanders, who lives here," she said. "But she had to go to the store, so we are waiting for her."

"In the closet," said Roland.

"We thought you were someone breaking into the house," said Griffin. It would almost have been believable, if she hadn't followed it with a questioning look to her grandmother, as if asking how she had done. Her grandmother closed her eyes, pursed her lips, and shook her head.

"Right," said Roland.

"You can't prove otherwise," said Delphine.

As much as he hated to admit it, she was probably right. It would have been a stretch.

He looked at Griffin but pointed at Delphine again. "You say this woman is your grandma?"

Griffin nodded and smiled.

"Anyone know why there's half a box of bullets here?" he asked next.

"G-ma likes to hunt," Griffin explained without hesitation, like she was now on a roll.

Roland hated to burst her bubble. "With a gun that shoots nine-millimeter bullets?"

"It's not unheard of," said Delphine.

Dammit if she wasn't right about that too. It was certainly a long shot, but still possible. "I need a raise," he said.

"What was that?" asked Griffin.

He just shook his head.

"We could easily make the case that you entered the house illegally," Delphine continued.

They sat and stared at the table some more.

"Truce?" he asked, and the older woman nodded.

He asked them twice more about the items on the table, but the first time Griffin said they were things that one of the ladies was trying to sell on eBay, and the second time Delphine said they didn't have to answer him.

Roland stood up from the table. "Well, we can all leave then," he said, pointing to the door.

"Oh, we can't go anywhere," said Delphine. "As I said, Marge told us to wait here for her until she got back from the store." She and Griffin didn't move from their chairs. "But you can go."

"I don't have time for this," he mumbled. "Don't get into any more trouble, okay?"

"Are you talking to me or her?" asked Griffin, tilting her head toward Delphine.

"Either. Both. Whatever," he snapped.

"We'll think about it," said Delphine as he closed the door.

As he walked down the stairs, her response finally hit him. Under other circumstances he'd go back in and set her straight about being a smart-ass to a detective, but he didn't feel like dealing with her anymore. He'd just have to let her think she'd won this round.

CHAPTER 21

"That was kind of fun," Griffin said after Roland left.

"He seems nice," said Delphine, looking at her granddaughter.

"What's that supposed to mean?"

"Nothing. You should have locked the door after you let me in."

"I guess you should have checked that I locked the door," said Griffin. It was a weak defense, she knew. The look her grandma gave her indicated that she agreed.

Delphine picked up the box of bullets.

"The Blingsters didn't leave too many clues behind, I guess," said Griffin.

"The who?"

"G-ma says the name of her gang of canasta players is called the Blingsters."

"Ladies who get together to play cards don't call themselves gangs," countered Delphine.

Griffin smirked. "You should see her play bridge with her team in Oklahoma."

"Point taken," said her grandmother.

"Where could they have gone?"

Delphine remained silent, turning the box over several times in her hands, lost in thought. The loose bullets rattled and clinked around inside the container.

Griffin frowned. "A box of nine-millimeter bullets doesn't exactly scream 'I went to a party in Palm Beach,' does it."

"Clearly you haven't been to any parties in Palm Beach," said Delphine.

"True." But not helpful. Griffin's stomach growled. All the sneaking around made her hungry.

"My sentiments exactly," said Delphine, in reference to the noise. "What's good to eat around here?"

"I know just the place."

Fifteen minutes later, they sat at a table in Little Moe's Diner.

"Don't get the smoothie," said Griffin as she looked over the menu.

"All right," said Delphine. "Are you sure this place is okay?" She looked doubtfully at her sticky menu and the worn Formica tabletop.

"Oh sure, it's pretty good," said Griffin.

There were more people in the diner this time; the place was maybe half full. The ice machine still hadn't been fixed and was making its usual horrible sounds.

"Charming ambiance," said Delphine.

"Do you like burgers? They're delicious."

"I'm a vegetarian, dear."

"Oh."

Alice was working that night, but instead of a Dolly Parton wig, this time she was wearing a Gidget-style hairdo, complete with pink headband and poofy hair, the ends of which flipped up toward the ceiling.

Delphine ordered a vegan club sandwich and Griffin got the breakfast scramble that her G-ma had ordered last time. As they waited, they looked around the room at the patrons. It was then that Griffin noticed Big Moe sitting in the only corner booth. No sign of Little Moe though. Maybe she was out shopping with G-ma. Big Moe caught her eye, and she could tell he recognized her.

"Everything okay, dear?" asked Delphine. "You look a little pale."

"Oh, uh, I just need some protein. Hey, how was your flight?"

Delphine launched into a story about a small child in the row behind her that kept throwing crayons over the seat and into her club soda. Or something like that; Griffin was only half listening. She tried to be a little less obvious as she watched Big Moe, who was sitting with two other men in the booth. They had on dark suits and Griffin's imagination made them out to be mobsters. But that was silly. They didn't live in Florida—everyone knew they all lived in New York or Chicago or cold, grim places like that.

Then an idea started to form in her mind. What if she could sell the big diamond that was back in the hotel safe to Big Moe? Ordinarily she wouldn't consider doing something like that, but ordinarily she also wouldn't consider plucking a huge gem out of someone's shag carpet and then keeping it. So there were multiple firsts occurring here. And she needed the money.

Tomorrow she would check her bank account balances and see how everything looked, just to be sure. With any luck, what happened at the car rental counter had been a fluke, and she still had plenty of money available. But what if she didn't? If Big Moe was a fence, he'd be stupid not to help her unload the incredible stone. Unless he knew about the diamond, and knew it was missing, in which case Griffin waltzing in with it would look mighty bad. But maybe it was a chance she was willing to take.

"Hey!" said Delphine.

"Oh! What?" Griffin said, startled.

"You haven't been listening to me."

"No? I mean no. I'm sorry. I was distracted. What were you saying?"

"I was saying that you seem to know that man over there." Delphine tilted her head toward Big Moe's table.

"I don't know him," said Griffin.

"You know which man I'm talking about?"

Griffin's mind raced. Busted! Should she tell Delphine about the Moes? She didn't want to reveal that yet, in case she decided to use their services, but was doubtful she could cover her mistake. "Um, I know no one at that table."

"Are you sure?"

Griffin nodded.

"Okay, because one of them seems to know you," said Delphine, inspecting her fingernails.

"Really? Which one?" asked Griffin.

Delphine let out a huff of frustration. "I'm too tired to play this game with you, Griffin. You don't want to tell me? Fine. But you asked me for help so if I find out you've withheld something that will aid us in recovering your lost grandma, I'm not going to be happy about it. Understood?"

Griffin nodded. She also promised herself she wouldn't look at Big Moe again and prayed that he wouldn't come talk to her. Despite Delphine's warning, Griffin decided to keep his identity to herself for now. It was doubtful he knew where Marge was anyway, she told herself.

Alice brought their food, and they ate in silence. Griffin wanted to know what they were going to do next but was afraid to ask her grandmother anything. Due to their lack of conversation, the meal went quickly and when Delphine finished her sandwich, she leaned back in her seat.

"We should get back on the road," she said.

"And go where?" asked Griffin.

"We'll decide that in the car."

CHAPTER 22

Roland returned to his car and reached for his vegan tacos after making sure that Griffin and Delphine left the beach house. Intuition told him to keep watching the place, and his hunch paid off when five minutes later, the black BMW X3 skidded to a stop out front and Marge, Elva, Daiyu, and Laverne hurried up the stairs. He wondered what the rush was. He also noticed that Laverne didn't have her cane anymore. She'd healed up mighty quick, or she'd faked it. He knew which way he was leaning.

Fifteen minutes after that, the four women clamored down the stairs dressed in evening gowns and fancy shoes, which made a real racket on the wooden steps.

Roland scarfed the last of his tacos, tossed the plate into the back seat (he kept the bag of candy up front though), and rolled up the windows. Then he pulled out his phone and called his captain.

"What are you doing calling so late?" said Captain Perez.

Roland checked the dashboard clock. "It's only nine," he said.

"Oh. Guess I must have dozed off. It's true what they say about turkey."

"I don't know what they say about turkey, sir, but listen, I really need some help tonight."

Perez yawned. "Yeah? Those old broads giving you a hard time?"

"No, sir. They're on the move. Something is definitely going on."

"What proof you got?"

Roland hesitated. "Still no proof. But they're headed out in evening wear, and I think they might be going to hit a party."

Captain Perez snorted. "Oh no, the seniors are going to a party! It's past their bedtime, call the police!" Before Roland could say anything, Perez said, "No, Benita, I'm not talking about your mother. Ow!"

"Look," said Roland. "You can make fun of me all you want, but something's going to happen and if you don't let me have some backup, you're going to regret it." His eyes went wide at the tone of his own words.

The captain was silent for a few beats. "Okay," he said. "Once you know the location, call down to the station and request three guys. That enough?"

"More than," said Roland. "Thanks, Rogelio."

"That's Captain to you," said the captain.

"Yes sir, thank you."

"One more thing," said Perez.

"Sure," said Roland, not feeling sure.

"If this doesn't pan out, you'll never hear the end of it."

"Understood, sir."

By the time he hung up, Marge, Elva, and Laverne had piled into Marge Flanders' sinfully beautiful Mercedes and were backing out of the carport. Daiyu had already gotten into her X3 and peeled out again and was probably halfway to New York by now.

He started the engine and followed as the Mercedes pulled away from the house, making sure to keep his headlights off until they turned onto a street with more traffic.

He liked tailing people. It was always a challenge, and over the years he'd gotten good at it. There was less of it to do than most people realized—three-quarters of his job was paperwork. But it was a nice night, with mild humidity and clear skies, perfect for a drive. He grew excited at the thought of this hunch panning out. It just had to; he wouldn't be able to face Rojas or Captain Perez if it didn't.

Roland followed the ladies onto the freeway and almost lost the Mercedes as Marge gunned the engine and the car took off down the road going at least ninety. It required all his concentration to keep up with her as she wove in and out of traffic. He hadn't had this much fun in a long time.

Once they were off the freeway, Marge slowed down, and they drove another few minutes until Roland followed the Mercedes through the open gates of a private neighborhood. He watched from down the street as they parked and made their way to a brightly lit mansion and disappeared inside.

Roland had to drive past the house and turn around again before he could find a parking space. The other cars on the street put his police vehicle to shame and, worse than that, made it obvious to anyone paying attention that he definitely did not belong there. But he was the one with the badge, so they could all just suck it.

CHAPTER 23

Griffin got behind the wheel of her tiny rental car and waited as Delphine tapped on her phone. Griffin tapped on the steering wheel.

"Should we drive around and hope we miraculously find something interesting?" Griffin felt frustrated. She wanted to take action but had no idea what that action should be.

"Let's go toward the freeway," said Delphine. Griffin pulled up the map app on her phone, started the car, and pulled out of the diner parking lot.

"Do you still have that nice policeman's card?" Delphine asked.

"Nice?"

Griffin caught her grandmother giving her a pitying look and only then realized it had been a sarcastic comment.

"Yes, I have it," she said. "It's in the front, medium-sized, left-hand pocket on the outside of my purse."

"Goodness, that's a lot of pockets," Delphine said, fishing out Rolly's business card. Within seconds she was back on her phone again.

Delphine continued her silence as Griffin drove. Griffin felt like she was the one asking everyone questions all the time. Why was she the last to know everything? It was frustrating, and her patience was wearing thin.

"Did you get some bad news on your phone?" she asked, hoping her grandmother would start talking. "Aliens took over the House of Representatives, perhaps?"

"What? No," said Delphine. Suddenly her eyes darted across the windshield and then met Griffin's. "You're going the wrong way. Make a U-turn and head toward the freeway. And step on it."

They should have taken G-ma's Mercedes for as fast as Delphine made Griffin drive. She felt bad for the rental car—the thing felt like it hadn't been built to be pushed above 45 mph. They rode for a while in silence again, and Delphine still wouldn't take her eyes off her phone. When they passed under a freeway sign pointing to Key Biscayne, Griffin started to get worried. Well, more worried. Where on earth were they headed? There was no point in asking because she knew she wouldn't get an answer. She just kept driving as Delphine gave more directions.

"What does Rolly's card have to do with where we're going?" Griffin asked, unable to keep from asking a question anyway.

"Nothing," said Delphine. "I wanted to look up a few things about him, that's all."

"I have a feeling you don't mean you wanted to check out his social media pages." Although maybe Griffin would do that sometime. What did she have to lose by looking? It wasn't like her husband cared.

"You are correct," said Delphine.

"Sure, because you have the authority and the means to dig into someone's past right from your cell phone."

"Yes," said Delphine.

"Oh. Did you find out anything good?"

"Depends on what you think 'good' is."

She hoped Delphine would elaborate further, but she didn't.

After a few more miles they exited the freeway and drove down a well-tended road with palm trees lining the median.

"Turn there." Delphine pointed to a narrow street leading into a residential area. They passed through an open gate that didn't close behind them.

"Nice security," said Griffin, checking her rearview mirror.

A minute later, they were parked on a street lined with huge mansions. Griffin caught sight of the ocean behind the homes on their right, the waves sparkling with moonlight.

"These houses are incredible," she said.

"Not exactly Palm Beach, but still nice," agreed Delphine. "What else do you see?"

They'd parked the rental car in between a late-model Alfa Romeo SUV and a vintage Porsche 911.

"All the cars on my wish list?" asked Griffin.

"And?"

"Not a lot of available on-street parking?"

"Someone is having a party."

Right on cue, a couple walked past them on the sidewalk, the woman in a red beaded evening dress and the man in a tux. They looked to be about G-ma's age, or slightly younger.

"Unless we're kitchen staff, we're underdressed."

"Let's go for a stroll down the street," said Delphine.

"Yeah, well, I think we're underdressed for that too."

They got out of the car, and Delphine took Griffin's arm as they followed a respectable distance behind the fancy couple. About five houses down, the pair turned onto a walkway and through an open iron gate, behind which was the largest house on the street. Griffin and Delphine kept walking.

"This doesn't look good," said Griffin, always ready to state the obvious.

"No, it doesn't."

They walked in silence and at the end of the street, they came to a marina where they stood looking out at the yachts.

"Must be nice to have a life like this," Griffin said.

Delphine shrugged. "That's what they want us to think."

Griffin thought of Brian then, and how over the last few years he'd become obsessed with having a life like these people had. His insistence that they buy a house way too big for the two of them (and still way too big even if they had five kids—which was definitely *not* on Griffin's to-do list) had been troubling to her, and the brand-new, seven-series BMW he'd just purchased seemed an unnecessary upgrade from his five-year-old Infiniti. She was perfectly happy in her Subaru, which she expected to last until her retirement. Which was kind of an irrelevant marker of time these days since she was out of work and had nothing to retire from.

Even before the whole buy-a-new-big-house thing, his demeanor had changed. All he did was talk about money. He was an accountant, and she was in finance, so they talked about money a lot anyway, but he was obsessed with getting more. More, more, more. He must have figured that hooking up Shelby Wafer was a better strategic move than staying with Griffin.

Well, she supposed he was getting what he wanted now. She looked around at the houses again. Maybe it wasn't so great here after all. Still, she wondered how far the diamond in her hotel room safe would get her toward one of the cars on her wish list.

Delphine let out a little cough, and Griffin realized her grandmother had been watching as she'd gotten lost in her thoughts. She smiled, embarrassed at having tuned out.

"A life like this isn't everything, you know," said Delphine. "In fact, I'd say it's overrated."

"I know," said Griffin, sounding sadder than she wanted to. Maybe she could tell Delphine what was going on. Later. She sighed.

"It'll be all right," said Delphine.

Griffin wished her grandmother was talking about her life, but she knew Delphine had referred to Marge. "I guess. Thanks." She took a deep breath and looked back at the big party house. "Is G-ma in that house with her roommates?"

"Yes."

"Seriously, how do you know these things? I can't believe you have the means to do it. What agency are you working for?"

Delphine dipped her chin and looked Griffin in the eye. "I'm retired, remember?"

Griffin snorted, and Delphine laughed.

"I really am retired," Delphine continued. "Sort of. I did a little tracking to get us here."

All mirth left Griffin's face and she stared at her grandmother, uncomprehending.

Delphine put her hands on Griffin's arms, turning her around to face the way they'd come. "See that car right there?" She pointed over Griffin's shoulder to the opposite side of the street.

And there was Roland Magnusson's car. It was facing away from them, but even so, the figure sitting in the driver's seat looked a lot like Roland Magnusson.

CHAPTER 24

"How … How did you know he would be here?" asked Griffin, looking between her grandmother and Roland's car.

"Again, some things are better left a mystery," was all Delphine said.

"Whatever. We walked right past his car and I didn't notice!"

"You just need more practice. I'm not sure he noticed either."

"That just means both of us need more practice," said Griffin.

Delphine laughed. At least Griffin could provide her grandmother with some entertainment.

"So now what?" Griffin asked.

"I'm not sure we should crash the party," said Delphine, putting a finger to her lips in thought. "But let's go see what Mr. Magnusson is up to."

They walked back along the side of the street where Rolly was parked. His Crown Vic was wedged in between a Mercedes Maybach with dealer tags and a Bentley convertible.

Griffin pointed at his car. "Only law enforcement would drive a car like that."

"One would hope," said Delphine.

"I was a top financial analyst for the FBI," Griffin announced. She wasn't sure why she felt the need to defend her occupation to

Delphine. Maybe, despite what her grandma had said about wealth being overrated, they were walking among cars that cost more than what she made in a year, and she wanted her grandmother to understand that she'd chosen a profession that was supposed to help others. She hadn't put the pursuit of wealth above everything else. Or maybe she was simply trying to make herself feel better about the choices she'd made. The cars lining the street really were on her fantasy wish list.

"Yes," said Delphine. "And we'd had such high hopes for you too."

"What's that supposed to mean?"

"Nothing, dear."

By this point they'd made it to Rolly's car, and Griffin heard the door locks release. Delphine got in the front seat, Griffin got in the back.

"Are you tired of us yet, Rolly?" Griffin asked him.

"Would you leave if I said yes?" he said.

"I'm just saying we should have carpooled over," said Griffin.

"My name is not Rolly," he said, shooting Griffin a look of disdain.

"Right."

"Anyway," he said, "what in god's name are you two doing here?"

"We followed you," Griffin said, trying to sound nonchalant.

His mouth dropped open and he looked at Delphine. "I'm assuming you had something to do with this."

"I will neither confirm nor deny that." Delphine maintained her usual air of casualness.

Now Roland swung his head to Griffin in the back seat. "Who is this lady?"

"I told you, she's my grandma."

He rubbed a hand along his jawline, which was covered in dark brown stubble flecked with silver. Then he propped one elbow on the window opening of his car door and draped his other hand across the steering wheel. He looked so ... rugged.

Unlike Brian, who insisted on waxing everything and slept with a hair bonnet.

To distract herself from thinking any more about the man who would soon become her ex-husband if she had any say in the matter, she looked around the back of the car. "How come you don't have a cage thingie for prisoners back here?" asked Griffin.

"Because it's an unmarked car?" Roland asked back, in a tone she didn't appreciate.

"You should know that, dear," said Delphine.

Roland looked at Delphine. "Why should she know that? And wait, how do you know that?"

"I know things," said Delphine.

"See, that's just it," said Roland. "I don't know how you know these things. I can't tell what side of the law either of you are on. You could be here as accomplices to those friends of yours, for all I know."

Griffin hadn't thought of that, once again cementing her status as an amateur. "We're harmless," she said.

Delphine barked a laugh. "Speak for yourself!"

"I'm just saying. Okay, Rolly, so I used to work for—"

"One more word out of you and I'll shoot," said Delphine.

Roland gripped the steering wheel tighter. "This should be obvious to you but in case it's not, do not pull your weapon in this vehicle."

"No promises," said Delphine.

"Could you two please stop this weird competition thing you've got going on?" said Griffin.

"Griffin, please keep quiet and don't complicate matters. This nice young man doesn't need to know anything about our business."

"Oh, see, that's where you're wrong," said Roland. "I need to know everything about your business. For example, I need to know if you're planning to shoot me here in my own car."

"Do we look like we'd shoot you?" Griffin asked.

"You, not so much." Then he nodded toward Delphine. "But she looks like she'd take someone down for incorrect grammar."

Now Griffin laughed. "The grammar police! Haha, good one Rolly!"

Roland shook his head and looked out the window. The car became quiet, and Griffin wondered why her grandmother was being so closemouthed about their backgrounds. She couldn't come up with a good reason. It must have been to serve some purpose that Griffin wasn't aware of because Delphine was the kind of person to have a reason for everything she did.

"How did the two of you first meet?" asked Delphine.

"Rolly bought me a beer at a Cheesecake Factory," explained Griffin.

"Funny," said Roland, not laughing.

Griffin leaned back in the back seat. She slouched down and began to feel sorry for herself. Here she was, in an unmarked police car in Key Biscayne, Florida, with a good-looking cop and her grandma. And they were all spying on her other grandma. She should have been home reading a book. But now all that was gone—her house, even the books. She had no place to go back to whenever all this was done. Hopefully she would figure something out.

The neighborhood had been quiet all this time, but now music from a live band floated through the air; they must have been set up in the backyard of the party house and were coming off a break. Griffin imagined champagne and fancy snacks, and candles set up around a big pool. A life a million miles away from the back seat of a police-issue Crown Vic.

Delphine's gaze moved from Griffin to Roland, then to the street. Roland picked up a pair of binoculars and held them to his eyes.

"Are those night vision binos?" asked Delphine.

"No," said Roland, tossing them back onto the bench seat. "I can't see sh—I mean jack."

"Maybe I should go in," said Delphine. She tapped an index finger against her cheek in thought.

"Then I'm going too," announced Griffin.

"No!" said Delphine and Roland at the same time.

She crossed her arms like a petulant child in the back seat. In a way, she was one. "Well you can't go either, you're not dressed appropriately," she said to her grandmother.

Delphine reached into her purse and whipped out a silky black scarf that had strands of shimmery silver woven into it. She wrapped it around her neck and just like that, her dark blazer and slacks received a party-worthy upgrade.

"Why should I let you go in there?" Roland asked Delphine.

This was it! Her grandmother was finally going to reveal her credentials, or top-secret identity, or alter-ego or whatever. Griffin would finally know who Delphine worked for and what she did. They were going talk shop.

"Because you can't stop me," was all Delphine said before she got out of the car and disappeared down the street.

"Should I worry about her?" he asked Griffin.

"Nope."

CHAPTER 25

Delphine walked through the oversized front doors of the mansion and gripped her handbag a little tighter. She made an effort to lengthen her spine—these days she wasn't getting any taller (or even staying the same height, sadly). Also, walking as if she owned the room made her feel like she owned the room. Years of experience had provided her with an extensive bag of tricks.

First thing on her list was to locate Marge, without Marge noticing. It was too soon to make herself known; she wanted to observe and get the lay of the land. She only wished she knew what the other three women looked like. For that reason, it would have been nice to have Griffin with her, but she couldn't take chances. Griffin wasn't trained like she was, and sending someone into a situation they weren't ready for was a recipe for disaster. Years of experience had taught her that too.

She nodded to a few partygoers as she walked farther into the house, coming to a huge living space with marble floors and a high ceiling. Large glass doors had been slid open to create the sensation that the entire living room was outdoors. In a large yard surrounded on two sides by rows of palm trees, about twenty or thirty tables were set up around a long pool, and a twelve-piece band played on a raised platform down at the deep end. The space backed up to the ocean, where a superyacht sat moored at the dock.

Delphine was used to traveling in wealthy circles, although she herself chose to live a more modest lifestyle. But she'd spent enough time in the company of the ultra-rich that it didn't faze her much anymore. She scanned the guests in the backyard and didn't see anyone who looked like how she remembered Marge, so she tried the other parts of the house where guests had congregated—the large kitchen, the second large living room, the large library, and the third large living room. As she entered this last area, she spotted Marge. The woman looked much different than she'd remembered, but it had been a while and she'd never seen Marge in party clothes.

The woman wore a long, dark-blue sequined dress that contrasted beautifully with her short, white hair. The red lipstick was a nice touch too, and something about her appearance made Delphine almost wistful for days gone by. Oh well, she had sown her wild oats. And in a way, she understood what Marge saw in all this. But that was no license to steal, if that's what was really going on.

Right next to Marge stood a very short woman with jet-black hair wearing a red silk dress and black flats. She must have been one of "canasta players." Delphine stood in the hallway and watched the women as they talked with two men in tuxedos. They laughed at something the small woman said, and then one man took Marge's arm and they all began to walk toward Delphine.

Delphine turned to head down the hall but bumped into something very big and very solid.

"Excuse me," it said, and reached out two log-like arms to hold her steady as she wobbled.

Delphine looked up. And then looked up higher, and higher still, until she found an age-appropriate, nice-looking man's head at the top of his tree-trunk body. Based on the cut of his tuxedo, she determined he was a guest and not security. That was lucky.

"Thank you," she said, and tried to extricate herself from his branches. She looked into the living room. Marge and her friends were coming closer.

"Say, would you like to dance?" asked the tree.

Delphine turned her head toward the wall as the four people walked past her and the tree. Marge and her gentleman friends went in the direction of the backyard, but the smaller woman in the red dress went the other way.

"Sure, I suppose that would be fine," Delphine said. She watched as the woman in red headed to the large marble staircase by the front door and slipped between two stanchion posts meant to keep guests on the lower level. Then she disappeared up the steps.

The tree took Delphine's elbow, and they followed Marge and her two friends outside.

Marge and one of the men walked onto the parquet dance floor that had been set up on the patio, while the other man lowered his head in disappointment and made a beeline to the buffet.

Delphine and her dance partner waited for the next song to begin. She knew she needed to make some decent conversation with the man, but she felt distracted by Marge. Maybe she was losing her touch.

"I'm Kristoff," said her partner.

"Philomena," she said.

"I will call you Philo for short, like the dough, haha," said Kristoff.

The band started playing a Sinatra classic, "Fly Me To The Moon." Kristoff took Delphine by the waist, and off they went. He was surprisingly light on his feet for someone so large.

"Are you friends with Peter and Luanne?" he asked.

"No."

Marge and her companion had started dancing also.

"How is it that you know Peter and Luanne?" asked Delphine.

Kristoff started in on a tale about venture capitalism, private jet rental, and retiring from a private contracting firm that did business in the Middle East. Somewhere in there was golf with Peter at the club. Delphine made all the appropriate sounds of being impressed by his wealth and influence, and as she expected, he made no effort to ask her anything about herself. Any other day Delphine would've been all ears though, listening for tidbits of intrigue and espionage, but today she needed to save Griffin's other grandmother, the one who was a jewel thief, from self-destructing. Hopefully that was possible, she mused.

The song ended and the next one began before Delphine had a chance to excuse herself from Kristoff's grip, so she continued to dance with him and keep an eye on Marge.

Two women dancing together made their way closer to Marge. One was a large woman with red hair, the other was smaller with white, longer hair. Delphine was all for people partnering up however they wanted to, both on and off the dance floor, but something about this duo seemed odd. When the women were right next to Marge, Marge leaned in and whispered something in her dance partner's ear. And then it happened.

A woman in a gold lamé dress appeared on the dance floor and marched right up to Marge's dance partner and slapped him in the face. That must have been the wife. Then the three of them stood there arguing, eventually joined by the two women dancers. The tiny black-haired woman in the red dress was now back on the scene, with a black satchel over her shoulder, much too large to be appropriate for evening wear. Those four women had to be the Blingsters.

Delphine watched as the husband, the wife, the white-haired lady, and Marge all talked over each other. The white-haired lady gave the wife a little shove while the red-haired woman stole the necklace right off the jealous woman's neck.

"So then I decided to buy a premiere league soccer team," Kristoff was saying, and Delphine realized she'd been inattentive to her partner. How ironic.

"Oh, that's fascinating!" she said, recalling for a moment the book that had come out in her younger years, *Fascinating Womanhood*. Her own grandmother had suggested she read it. The premise of the book was basically, fake interest in a man and you will be rewarded. Delphine had never read it. She'd never been into those kinds of rewards.

When she looked back to Marge, the conversation had turned into a full-blown argument, and their voices were louder. They were on the verge of creating an even bigger scene.

"Would you excuse me?" Delphine asked, interrupting Kristoff's monologue.

"You don't have to go just yet," he said, smiling at her.

She recognized that smile. While his words could have been taken as charming, there was an underlying threat to his statement that she knew all too well. Little did he know that what was meant to not bode well for her, would end up not boding well for him, if he didn't behave like a gentleman. "If you don't let me go, I will kick you in the onions so hard you won't be able to think straight for a week."

And that was the last she ever saw of Kristoff.

By the time she had made it halfway over to the arguing group, it was already too late. A scuffle had begun, and Marge had fallen into the pool. Delphine knew there was nothing she could do at that point, and the last thing she wanted was to be associated with Marge and her three accomplices. She turned right around and left the house, not waiting to see anything more.

CHAPTER 26

"Did you know these cars are prone to exploding?" asked Griffin from the back seat of the Crown Victoria.

"You know nothing about prisoner partitions, but you know the car might explode?" asked Roland with more than a hint of snark.

Griffin ignored him. "There have been at least thirty law enforcement officers killed in this kind of car. Five of those were right here in Florida."

"If this is your idea of small talk, maybe we should just enjoy each other's silent company," he said.

"Okay," said Griffin.

But he couldn't help himself.

"What's your grandma's deal?" he asked, turning in his seat now to look at Griffin.

"Which one?"

He scratched the back of his head. Honestly, he wasn't sure which one he had meant, but he chose one. "The one who threatened to kick my ass at least twice tonight."

"That's not my story to tell," she said, not meeting his gaze.

"So in other words, you don't know."

"Am I that obvious?"

"Yep."

He checked the street again, but everything was quiet. Still, he had that feeling. This was it, and he was glad that he'd finally gotten his captain to listen to him and give him some help.

"I used to be in the FBI," Griffin said out of nowhere.

"You? FBI?" asked Roland, sounding incredulous. He almost let out a laugh but caught himself.

"It's not that hard to believe," snapped Griffin.

"It kind of is," he said.

"I was a financial analyst. I didn't run around with a gun and chase people and stuff. I chased the money. People like you wouldn't get very far without people like me." She crossed her arms and leaned back in the seat, but the backrest was farther away than she realized, and she fell sideways.

Without thinking, Roland reached an arm into the back of the car and offered her his hand. But she refused his assistance. When she had righted herself, Roland said, "People like you wouldn't get very far without people like me either."

She glared at him until he shrugged and turned back to face the windshield. He heard the back door of the car open and then close, and she joined him in the front seat.

"Do you have anything to eat in here?" Griffin asked.

He pointed to the brown paper bag on the seat between them. "Snacks," he said. "Help yourself."

She rooted around in the bag and pulled out a package containing two peanut butter cups. His favorite, and he was sorry to see them go.

"So you were FBI. Why did you leave?" he asked.

"They let me go."

"What for?"

"I have no idea," she admitted through a mouthful of peanut butter cup.

"Maybe it was because you ran around telling people their car was going to explode," he offered. All that got him was a glare. "They have to tell you something."

"I'll get right on that as soon as I figure out the rest of my problems, like…" She stopped talking and eating.

"Like what?"

"It's nothing," she said.

"You said that earlier. I'm not buying it. Come on. What's wrong?"

"Okay fine, I'll tell you. My husband called while we were at the Cheesecake Factory to tell me that he's run off with our real estate agent. He put all my stuff in storage and seems to have cleaned out our bank accounts. That's what's wrong." She tossed an uneaten peanut butter cup back into the snack bag and he went in after it.

"He told you in a phone call?" he asked, and she nodded. "Harsh."

"What a jerk," she said, crossing her arms.

"What did you say to him?" Roland imagined her giving this guy a piece of her mind and a tiny spark ignited somewhere in his heart.

"I … I didn't say anything." Griffin looked shocked, like she couldn't believe her own words. "I didn't say a damn thing."

"That doesn't sound like you. Not that I know you very well," he added.

"I'm just so tired," she said, and sighed.

"I know what you mean." He leaned back and popped the entire peanut butter cup in his mouth. Maybe he and Griffin were cut from the same cloth.

"Yeah, well, tomorrow I'll call that jerk and rip him a new one!" Griffin announced.

"That's kind of extreme, isn't it?"

"Remember, he cleaned out our bank accounts."

"Oh, right," said Roland. "In that case, rip away."

She nodded.

"I'm sorry," he said.

"I don't need your apology," said Griffin.

Roland looked down at his hands. She hadn't sounded mad

when she said it, but maybe she was right. Had been presumptuous to say that? He was so out of practice with all this crap. No wonder his own marriage was starting to feel like a sham.

Griffin looked at him and their eyes met. "But thanks."

"You're welcome."

They sat a little while in silence, looking out the front of the car toward the party house. "If it makes you feel any better, I got offered a job as a stripper yesterday," said Roland.

"Really?"

"Honest to god. But I didn't have my own nightstick and I think they were looking for men who had all their own equipment." As soon as he said it, his face turned red at the unintended double entendre. He was glad it was dark in the car.

"I don't know what to say to that," said Griffin.

"I guess I should have asked about benefits," he said.

"Was that event a career low, or a career high for you?"

"I'm not sure yet."

They laughed.

"I really am sorry about your husband though. He sounds like a real ass hat."

"I'm starting to wonder if he was one from the very beginning and I didn't notice, or if he turned into one somewhere along the way," she said. Then she shrugged. "But maybe it doesn't matter since, well, here we are."

What she said rang true for Roland too. Not that Christina was an ass hat. But maybe they had been incompatible from the get-go, and he hadn't seen it. "Here we are," he agreed.

Griffin took the bag of snacks and looked through it again. "Where's the other peanut butter cup?"

"Right here," he said, and pointed to his belly. She looked disappointed. "Sorry. Again."

He was about to apologize for his earlier suggestion to get together in Texas sometime when they heard a commotion from up the street.

"Uh-oh," said Griffin. "I have a very bad feeling about this."

Roland didn't need his binoculars to see two white-haired ladies and a large redheaded woman rushing down the walkway from the party house. When they got to the sidewalk, they turned toward his car.

"That's them. Three-fourths of them, anyway. Why are they all yelling at each other?" asked Griffin.

Roland leaned forward over the steering wheel, as if getting that much closer would help him hear what they were saying. He couldn't understand any of the words the ladies were slinging at each other, but the tones of annoyance and accusation were unmistakable.

"Where's Smitty?" asked Griffin.

"Who?" asked Roland.

As soon as the word left his mouth, the tiny, silk-clad ninja raced down the sidewalk and right past the other three ladies. She looked like she was clutching a small crossbody bag to her chest.

Finally, this was it. All his hard work was about to pay off, and all the chiding would finally stop. Hopefully.

He touched his left ear with his index finger, like they did in the movies—another 'Hawaii 5-O' moment.

"Whirlpool side-by-side!" he said, and jumped out of the car and ran toward the group of women.

CHAPTER 27

Griffin wanted to ask why Roland was so excited about refrigerators, but he'd jumped from the car before she could open her mouth. She watched as Big El looked up and noticed Roland barreling at her, but before she could warn the others, three men dressed all in black and sporting bulletproof vests descended on the scene and had the ladies surrounded on the sidewalk.

"G-ma!" Without thinking, Griffin opened the passenger side door of the car to run across the street. A hand caught her arm and stopped her in her tracks.

"Griffin, no."

Delphine's directive stopped her cold. She looked at her grandma, amazed at what she was hearing. Didn't Delphine want to help? Maybe it was all a big misunderstanding, or what if G-ma got hurt? "We have to do something!" Griffin pleaded.

"There is nothing we can do here. Let's go." Delphine gently pulled on her arm until Griffin gave up.

They stood in the street for a moment and watched Roland wrestle with Smitty, who seemed to put up more of a fight than he'd bargained for. Once he subdued her he looked through her bag, and the four men handcuffed everyone. Including Marge.

"How am I going to explain this to Dad," said Griffin.

"I'll take care of it," said Delphine, and they walked arm-in-arm back to the rental car.

Griffin couldn't hear what the cluster of people on the other side of the street were saying until Smitty's roar ripped through the night air with an explosive, "I want a lawyer!"

Griffin drove and Delphine gave her directions to Roland's police station. How her grandmother knew which one it was seemed to be just one more item on a long list of things that were above Griffin's pay grade.

"Could you have gotten a tinier car?" asked Delphine. She was by no means a tall woman, yet she looked like she was crammed into the passenger seat. Her knees almost touched the dash.

"It's all I could afford." She turned on the car radio, which blasted them with tinny Latin pop music.

"Really?" Delphine turned the radio back off. "Is everything okay?"

"You mean besides G-ma getting arrested for lord knows what and being stuck halfway across the country with no … with no…"

"With no what?"

Griffin pounded the steering wheel in frustration. She was going to have to tell her family at some point, and she might as well start with Delphine. It had been easier to tell Roland; he was a neutral party. Family was different. But it was time to rip the band-aid off.

"Brian is cheating on me," she blurted. Delphine didn't say anything, so Griffin stole a quick glance at her. "You don't seem all that surprised."

Delphine took a deep breath before she spoke. "I'm so sorry. Has it been going on for very long?"

"I don't know. Maybe a few months?" Griffin told Delphine everything, from describing Shelby Wafer to confessing her bank accounts were empty. Saying it all out loud to her grandmother made it more real somehow, and she wiped her eyes with the sleeve of her cardigan.

"Come on, let's stop for a snack," said Delphine.

"What about G-ma?"

"She's not going anywhere."

Delphine tapped on her phone a few times and gave Griffin directions to a nearby coffee house. They went in and ordered herbal teas and a cinnamon scone to share and sat at a table in the corner farthest away from the small stage. An acoustic band played slow, soulful renditions of Huey Lewis and the News hits. Sadly, they weren't very good—the cover band or the songs.

In a quiet voice, Griffin related the rest of what she knew to Delphine, which wasn't much.

"That little shit," said Delphine.

Griffin sniffed. "Just don't tell G-ma, okay? Or anyone else."

"Why not?"

"Because she's got enough on her plate right now. And it's private. It's embarrassing."

"Griffin, it is not embarrassing to discover your husband is a shit. It's not your fault that he strayed."

"It kind of is! I should have known. Or if I were more … interesting or whatever…" She thought about Shelby's curvaceous figure and fancy wardrobe.

"You are a very interesting person, Griffin. You're quiet, observant, and perhaps a little socially awkward, but who isn't from time to time? I know we haven't spent much time together, but I've been watching you, and I've always been interested in your career and who you have become. To be honest, though, you did a terrible job choosing a first husband."

"I know, Brian is an ass hat."

"A what?"

"Did you just say first husband?"

Delphine smiled but said nothing.

They drank their tea and finished off the scone, and Delphine said, "I won't say anything to Marge or your parents. How and when you tell them is your business. But you should say something."

"No," said Griffin. She was independent and proud of her

accomplishments, such as they were, and she didn't want her family's pity.

"Suit yourself," said Delphine. "But how about for the rest of our stay in this godforsaken state, you let me take care of the expenses, okay?"

"Normally I'd say no way, but right now I probably don't have a choice. I don't even know how I'm going to get my things out of storage in Fort Worth." She started sniffling again. What a sob story.

"Don't worry, we'll figure it out," said Delphine, putting a hand on Griffin's arm.

Griffin looked at her grandma's hand. It was showing its age, with a few wrinkles and age spots here and there. But it was an elegant hand, with slender fingers and manicured nails. She felt comforted. Maybe things would turn out all right. Maybe they would turn out better than if she'd stayed with Brian. Only one way to find out. And that was by doing the next thing and then the next, and to keep on going.

"Thanks, Delphine," said Griffin.

"That's what grandmas are for. Now let's go see what Marge is up to. They've probably got her fingerprinted by now."

CHAPTER 28

It was about 2 a.m. and Griffin had fallen asleep in a chair in Detective Magnusson's tiny office. She and Delphine were waiting for him to come back from filling out some paperwork, or whatever it was that detectives did once they got their man. Or in this case, four female, senior, alleged jewel thieves. Not even the overpowering smell of stale Fritos and Dial soap—which Roland insisted came in through the vents and was not a reflection of what he ate or bathed with—could keep her awake.

When they'd first gotten to the police station, G-ma was still being processed, and they waited in the lobby. Then Roland took Delphine back, and Griffin had to wait up front by herself. Finally she'd gotten to join Delphine in Roland's office, and now here they were, waiting some more.

Delphine woke her up with a gentle shake to her shoulder and handed her a tissue to wipe away the drool. Griffin was totally disoriented but once she could focus, Delphine was sitting next to her, smiling.

"You can go see her."

"Do I have to?" asked Griffin.

Delphine looked confused. "Excuse me?"

"No, sorry. I guess I didn't mean that. I'm just tired."

"Well buck up, kiddo, and go take your grandma's mind off her predicament."

That would be hard, Griffin reckoned, considering G-ma was sitting in a jail cell. "When can we spring her from the joint?" she asked as she got up and stretched.

"I'm working on it."

"And what does that entail?"

Delphine pursed her lips. "I'm not at liberty to say."

"What is it with this family?" mumbled Griffin. No one gave a straight answer about anything, and it was exhausting. She left Rolly's office and a uniformed officer escorted her to Marge's cell. There would be so many things about this trip that she would have a hard time explaining to her parents.

Griffin's chaperone led her through two sets of locked doors before depositing her in a cement hallway that had three small, barred cells along each side.

"How are you holding up?" Griffin asked as she stood outside one of the tiny cells, looking at Marge who sat on a bench on the far wall. The lighting was dim, but from a distance, her G-ma looked okay.

"How do I look like I'm holding up?" Marge snapped. She stood and came toward the bars.

Griffin looked her over more carefully as she came closer. Her mascara had run, giving her raccoon eyes, and her hair was "styled" as if she'd taken a long drive in a convertible. She was also missing one shoe, and she looked sort of … damp?

"Jeez, what did the police do to you?"

"They didn't do anything." G-ma sounded disappointed.

"But that's a good thing, right?"

Marge sighed. "I guess. I was kinda hoping to get frisked by that Detective Magnusson. He's a real hottie!"

Oh lord. "G-ma, why do you look so, um, disheveled?"

"Would you believe all this happened at that stupid party?

Smitty threw me in the dang pool." She picked up the hem of her sequined evening dress and wrung it out, leaving a small puddle on the cell floor. "I don't think I can put this thing in the dryer," she said. "Do you?" She tried to straighten out the section of dress she'd wrung out, but it stayed smooshed up in a wet wrinkled mess and some of the sequins were bent. The best years of that dress' life were behind it.

So much for Griffin's image of a swanky backyard affair. Instead of slow dancing in the dark and easy laughter over the tops of wine glasses, it had been her grandmother thrown in the pool by a tiny woman who by all accounts had the strength of a pro wrestler.

"Are you gonna get me out of here?" asked Marge.

"I think Delphine is working on it."

"Good," said Marge. "What the heck is she doing here, anyway? Hard to believe she happens to be in Florida on vacation."

"I called her," said Griffin. "There was no way I could keep up with you. I mean, you're in *jail*, G-ma!"

"Tell me something I don't know," snapped Marge, and Griffin realized she wasn't doing a very good job of taking her grandma's mind off her predicament. What on earth could they talk about though?

"Did you see that the Oklahoma City Thunder won last night?" asked Griffin.

"They played the Spurs, dear. Hardly counted as basketball."

"Oh."

"Say, have you heard anything about where Vern and the gang are?" asked Marge.

"Nope," said Griffin. "I'm assuming they're all getting their own lawyers or whatever."

"Do I need a lawyer?"

"You have something better—you have a Delphine."

"Oh yeah! She sure is a badass."

They stood in silence for a moment, and Griffin's curiosity got the better of her. "Why did you have bullets on your dining room table?"

"Those things? I don't know. They're Smitty's. I think she likes to go to the shooting range with one of her boyfriends. The one who's a retired police chief. Or maybe the mobster. I'm not sure, I keep getting them mixed up."

"They weren't for using in a robbery?"

Marge laughed. "Oh Griffy, you're too funny. Do we look like gun-toting baddies?"

"I don't know," Griffin admitted. "What happened tonight, G-ma?"

Marge looked around, as if to make sure no one would overhear them. They were still totally alone; the guard had left and the other ladies must have been in a different section of the jail. She came closer toward the bars, motioning for Griffin to come closer too.

"Well, it turns out those three ladies are real-life jewel thieves," she confessed. "I suppose I knew on some level, but I was having so much fun, going to fancy parties and whatnot."

"I can't believe my grandma is a criminal," Griffin mumbled.

"I said *they* are thieves! I never took anything myself. I was what you call one of those duck decoys."

"It's just decoy, I think."

"Right, sure. See, they liked to use me as a diversion, on account of my good looks. I just flirted with the men a little bit, you know? Laugh at their jokes, show them a little leg, that kind of thing. It was great fun! Then—and this is all hearsay because I never saw anything, mind you, I'm innocent—the wives of the men I flirted with would get super jealous and distracted, and *bingo bongo!* One of the Blingsters would sneak up and take whatever they could. They've got real nimble reflexes for their ages! Or so I hear."

Griffin tried to picture Big El sneaking up on someone. She couldn't.

"What is Smitty in charge of?" she asked.

"Smitty's the muscle, our enforcer. She's also real good at cracking safes, from what I understand. I've never seen her do it, I swear! And Vern, I think she's the mastermind of the group. Honestly, she's got a brain for crime and a bod built for sin!"

"I may regret asking, but how do you know that?"

"Well," said Marge, lowering her voice, "one night she asked me if I wanted to be in one of her love triangle thingies! I thought about it, because I've never tried that before, and who knows? It could be fun! It sure sounds like they have fun, since my bedroom is right next to hers, you know, and I hear everything that goes on in there. The other night she was entertaining two real good-looking fellers, and—"

Griffin closed her eyes tight and raised one hand. "Please stop talking now," she said.

"But it's a funny story," said Marge, trying to entice her granddaughter, but Griffin shook her head. "Anyway, the ladies thought about recruiting a man to help us, you know, some nice young thing, so we could use him to distract more ladies. I was thinking that Rolly of yours might have worked out pretty good."

Griffin imagined Roland sidling up to jewel-laden women at society parties and stealing them blind, and she laughed. "He probably would be good at that."

"You tell him if he ever wants to change careers, he should call me!" said Marge, seeming to have forgotten her troubles for the moment.

Griffin laughed again. If being a detective didn't work out, now he had two backup careers. That was two more than she had at the moment.

"All right. So anyway, what went wrong tonight?" Griffin asked.

"Tonight we got our wires crossed," continued G-ma. "And I might have misread one of the signs or something, I don't know for sure, and Smitty pushed me in the pool as a last-ditch distraction. Then we had to leave, of course, since I was wetter than a submarine with screen doors. Smitty said it was one of their best hauls ever, but then Detective Hottie McHotterson showed up with his goons, and now I'm ruined!"

It was possible G-ma was crying, but it was difficult to tell since her mascara was so smeared to begin with.

"Oh Griffy, how did all this happen? All I wanted was to take a little cruise, maybe eat a whole lot of free shrimp and dance with a retired car salesman or two. Now everything is a complete mess." She walked back across the cell and sat down heavily on the narrow metal bench.

"Did you tell Hottie—sorry, Rolly—all this?" Griffin said. "I mean the part about you not being very involved?"

"Yeah, and Delphine too."

"She sat in on your interview with the detective?" Of course she had, because the woman was omnipotent.

"Uh-huh, she knows the whole story."

"Wait here." Griffin turned to leave.

"Good one, Griffy. Where the heck am I gonna go?"

Griffin extracted herself from the holding cell area and made her way to Roland's office with conflicted feelings. Her G-ma seemed genuinely distraught, and a little afraid about her situation. But she also thought her new life was fun and adventurous. It was possible the other Blingsters were so good at deception that they had fooled Marge too and managed to keep her in the dark about what they were doing. Yes, that had to be it. Griffin knew her grandma. There was no way she was one of them.

When she made it back to Rolly's office, he was sitting behind his desk engaged in a staring contest with Delphine. Griffin sat down in the chair next to her.

"It sounds like she was only an accomp—" Griffin started.

"Griffin, please go get your grandma a crappy cup of coffee from that vending machine over there." Delphine jerked a thumb toward the room outside Rolly's office without breaking eye contact with him.

Griffin knew her grandmother didn't really want coffee, so she left them to it and milled around the tables in the common area, watching the proceedings in the office. The two of them sat there staring at each other, not saying a word. After ten minutes, Griffin decided she might need a snack because it looked like it was going to be an even longer night than it already had been.

CHAPTER 29

Delphine hated sending Griffin away like a small child, but she knew for a fact that her granddaughter was not a good negotiator. She'd read Griffin's FBI file and while she was a brilliant financial analyst, she wasn't quite up to speed on a few of the subjects that were important right now. Her presence would have made the standoff with Roland worse than it already was.

She sat with a straight spine in the chair in front of his desk. Roland leaned back and crossed his arms in front of his chest. Everything about his expression and posture indicated he was on the defensive. Delphine didn't want to be the bad guy, but she'd promised to help the family, and that was what she was going to do.

"We were all friends earlier this evening," she pointed out. "I don't see what's changed."

"Everything has changed!" said Roland, leaning forward. "You waltz in here and want to take over? This is my investigation, lady. I don't know you from Adam."

That was true, for the most part. She had been able to go over Roland's head and force him to let her sit in on Marge's questioning. She'd meant to be impartial during the proceedings, but that hadn't quite worked out and she'd ended up functioning more like Marge's lawyer, trying to keep the woman from saying too much. She had no filter! She would tell anyone anything she was thinking about everything.

"All you need to know is that I have one of the highest security levels in the country and can get you fired with one twenty-second phone call. But I wouldn't do that, because I'm nice. I'm just saying I could." She leaned back in her own chair now.

"Those four women back there are guilty as sin," he said, pointing in the direction of the jail cells.

"We don't know that."

Roland snorted.

"You heard what Marge said. She claims she didn't know what her friends were up to. And you've never seen her do anything. Daiyu Smith was the one left holding the bag, literally. It's her you want. And possibly Laverne."

"No. All four of them."

"Well then," Delphine said, "you leave me no choice." She got out her phone and looked up a number. It was a number she only used sparingly these days, because she was out of the business. Then again, one was never really out of the business.

Roland put his hands on his desk. "Are you making that twenty-second phone call?" he asked. She knew he hadn't meant to reveal his concern, but his voice had a hint of doubt in it now. She had him right where she wanted him. It was too bad they couldn't reach an agreement, but she hadn't expected it in the first place.

She hit the green button to place the call and smiled at him as she put the phone to her ear. "Hello, Richard? Yes, hi. I'm sorry to be calling you so late … Oh, sorry to hear you can't sleep! Have you tried chamomile tea? Anyway, I won't keep you. I just have one quick thing to discuss."

Roland started waving his hands in the air to get her to stop but she kept talking.

"Great. I was wondering if you could do me a favor. I'm going to hand the phone over to someone in a minute, and I'd like for you to tell them your usual spiel, all right?" Pause. Delphine laughed. "Oh my yes, it's the usual red tape, you know how it goes. Anyway, here he is." She stuck out her hand and Roland took the phone.

His eyes never left hers. "Yeah." Pause. "Detective Roland Magnusson, Largo Police." Pause. "Yes." Another pause. "Fine." Pause. "No, thank *you*, sir." He handed the phone back to Delphine with a scowl.

"Thank you so much, Richard. No, everything is fine. I'm on a little vacation and have some business to take care of. Yes, we should get together sometime soon, I agree. You have a new wife? Oh fabulous! I'd love to meet her. Okay, fine. Yes. Bye-bye!"

Delphine couldn't stand Richard and had no intention of following through on getting together with him and his latest wife who, if memory served, was his fifth. But Roland didn't have to know that.

"Now then," she said. "I believe you have some release paperwork to fill out."

CHAPTER 30

Griffin, Delphine, and Marge made it back to the hotel resort spa just after six in the morning. They were beat, but also hungry, so after a small room service breakfast, they climbed into bed (Marge and Delphine got the queen beds, Griffin used the roll-away bed that came with the suite) and tried to get some rest.

Around 10:30, Griffin woke up and couldn't get back to sleep; too many thoughts raced through her mind. Her two grandmothers were still out cold, so she decided to let them be. She changed her clothes and left the room with her purse, the keys to the rental car, and the giant diamond from the safe, still nestled in her sport socks and tucked into the depths of her bag.

Before she knew what was happening, she was on her way to Little Moe's Diner.

She walked into the restaurant with trepidation, unsure of why she was there. Well, she knew why she was there; she just wasn't sure she'd have the courage to go through with it.

There was no sign of either Moe. To pass the time, she took a seat in the booth she'd occupied with G-ma, ordered a sandwich and side salad from Alice, and got out her phone. First, she checked whether she still had access to her bank accounts. She did, but they were empty. Next, she looked up her credit card account. The card was charged to the limit and this month's payment was in danger of being overdue. Man, Brian really was a shit. She could kick herself for not having seen it sooner.

It took her a few minutes to locate her sport socks in her purse, tucked into an inside side pocket. (This one had a zipper for extra safety!) She didn't take the socks out of the bag but kept her hand inside her purse and felt the shape of the diamond with her fingers. Its weight and size helped her feel grounded, a reminder that everything would be all right. Just as soon as she sold it to get some cash. Alice brought her food and she continued to wait for the Moes.

She didn't have to wait long. About halfway through her meal, Big Moe entered the diner, dressed again in a pink polo golf shirt and brown slacks. Griffin wondered if it was the same shirt from before and if he'd gotten the bird poop stain out. She watched as he took a seat in the corner booth again. He was soon joined by Little Moe, who must have been in the kitchen.

The couple sat right next to each other and started making out. It wasn't a very romantic sight, and definitely more PDA than Griffin wanted to see. But something about it was also heartwarming. She imagined they'd been together a long time and were still passionate about each other. How freakin' cute. She wanted to throw her sandwich at them.

But she was here to do business, she reminded herself, not judge relationships.

While killing time at the police station, Griffin had found the matchbook from the diner as she searched her bottomless purse for change for the vending machine. She looked up the name on the cover, *Ramona Pescatelli*. That led her to social media, where she found photos of her and Big Moe together in exotic locations, some taken from their boat, the *Nude-O-Rama*. Most of the posted pictures were just scenery.

She also learned during her snooping that Big Moe's real name was Morris Pescatelli, and he was a podiatrist, with a practice in an office building not far from the diner. The two of them must use the diner and the podiatry practice to launder money. Which was an odd choice, in more ways than one. First off, anything related to medical practices dealt mostly in insurance reimbursements rather than cash. And also, who would be interested in feet enough to keep a podiatry practice running when you were bringing in money from stolen jewelry? Unless you were also running insurance scams…

That line of thought would have to wait for another day. Thanks to her idiot husband, she needed money, and these two seemed like the easiest place to get it from. Albeit the scariest. And the most morally questionable.

There was more than a small possibility that trying to sell a diamond of uncertain origins made her as much of a criminal as the Blingsters. But she had *found* the diamond, she told herself. She hadn't stolen it from someone, per se. Regardless, finding it in the carpet of someone's house, and then failing to return it to the people living there, was bad. Even if those people had stolen it before her. She kept trying to convince herself that this was a grey area—so grey that it would be okay if she sold it. But she couldn't shake the feeling that she was a criminal now too. From FBI analyst to jewel thief. How far she had fallen, in such a short time! But she needed the money, and here was a straightforward solution…

These were the thoughts that had woken her up so early and continued to zoom through her mind as she sat watching the Moes.

"Want another iced tea?" asked Alice, appearing out of nowhere. Today's hairdo was a blond bouffant, unmistakably an homage to the waitress Flo from the TV series *Alice*. These days *server* was the word of choice, but Flo had been 100% *waitress*.

"Um, yes please. I'm going to leave my table for a minute, but don't take away my food, okay?"

"Okay, hon."

Griffin watched the Moes huddled together in the booth. The conversation she'd overheard at the beach house flashed in her mind. It was possible they thought she was competition to them, that she would steal the Blingsters' business from them. That added another layer to the bean dip of her predicament, but she was desperate enough to take the chance. Besides, the Blingsters might be on a permanent hiatus.

They'd stopped their PDA and sat in quiet companionship. It was now or never. She made her move.

Right as she slid to the edge of the bench seat, one of the black-suited men who had been in the diner the day before came in and went straight to the Moes' booth. Griffin scooched back to the center of her seat and started to feel a bit clammy.

Dealing with other people—negotiating or talking to them in general, really—was difficult for her. She was a numbers person. She understood finance and leverage and bond coupons, logic and numbers. But people were another matter. They were almost as mysterious as … She couldn't think of anything more mysterious than people. The idea of going over to talk to the Moes was scary enough, but she wasn't sure she could do it with one of the dark-suited men there too. Her business was definitely not his business. Unless it was.

Alice brought another tea and Griffin took a bite of her sandwich while she contemplated. And as she chewed, the other dark-suited man entered the diner and went to the corner table too. Oh no.

Another bite of sandwich. Then some salad. A little more tea. Little Moe got up and left the booth, disappearing into the kitchen. The ice machine droned on, and Griffin felt like she was in a bad movie, like she was waiting for something awful to happen.

But if she waited too long, Big Moe might leave too. Okay, this was it. She was about to start sliding out of the booth when she heard a chime, indicating she'd gotten a text. It took her close to a minute to locate her phone in her purse.

G-ma: *Where are you, Griffy? We want to go to lunch!*
Griffin: *I'll be back soon, I'm at the bank.*

Pause.

G-ma: *Fine, we will go to the pool and enjoy the eye candy.*

Griffin rolled her eyes and put her phone away. This time she did manage to slide to the end of her seat, get up, and walk over to the corner booth. Little Moe had returned with a carafe of coffee and four cups and was seated next to Big Moe again. They all looked up at her as she approached. Which was when she realized she hadn't thought about what she was going to say.

Maybe it didn't seem so far-fetched that the FBI had let her go after all.

She got to the table and stood in front of them. Big Moe leaned back. "Yes?" he said.

"I, uh…" Griffin thought she might pass out. A few different scenarios of how this conversation might go played through her mind, and none of them ended well for her. "I just wanted to ask if you got that bird poop out of your shirt. You know, from the other day?"

The men in suits turned their skeptical gazes to Big Moe, who sat with fingers steepled on the tabletop.

"Is that so," he said. "You are here to ask me about bird poop?"

"Well, no. I mean, yes. No. I wanted to know if…"

Did they know she had the diamond?

She really needed the money.

Did they know the Blingsters were in jail? Well, all of them except Marge?

Did they think maybe she had something to do with their arrests? Surely they didn't think that. She didn't have anything to do with it, but she felt guilty anyway, for some reason.

"Spit it out, honey," said Little Moe.

"Yes," said Big Moe. "We are in the middle of a private conversation here, so what is your question?"

Griffin tried again. "If…"

"Is there something wrong with this lady?" asked one of the suits. He tapped a finger to his temple. "In the head?"

Big Moe looked at him. "Moe Junior, that is a very ableist thing to say."

"Sorry," said Moe Junior.

Big Moe looked at Griffin. "It appears that you do not have another question for me. But I have one for you. Do you know where Vern, Smitty, Big El, and Marge are?"

"Why would I know where they are? I don't know anything about where they are. Why would you think that?" Griffin tried to look innocent. But she really didn't know where three of them were, so technically she wasn't lying too much.

"One of them is your grandmother, is she not? Marge, I believe? You do not know where she is?"

"Oh, right, haha," said Griffin. "Well, you know Marge. It's almost impossible to keep track of where she is from minute to minute. I mean let's face it, she's a little bit nutso, right? Haha…"

The four people at the table looked at her and didn't seem to appreciate the humor. This had been a terrible, terrible idea.

"Oh gosh, is that the time? I'm late for a thing. So bye-bye then." She gave them a little wave and was about to turn on her heel when Big Moe spoke.

"Look, Griffin is it? To answer what seems to be your only question, no, I did not get the seagull excrement out of my shirt. It seems that a mercerized cotton and polyester blend fabric does not respond well to poopies."

"I'm sorry to hear that," said Griffin.

She noticed he'd clenched his fists now, and she made the executive decision to give up on trying to sell hot merchandise to a fence who might blame her for the arrest of four of his best customers. That had been too close for her comfort. Her life of crime just ended before it had a chance to begin. Old guy 1, Griffin 0.

CHAPTER 31

When she'd gotten back from the diner, the hotel suite was empty, so she put the sock-encased diamond back into the safe. She sat on the couch and reflected on her failed attempt at fencing jewels. Of course, she wouldn't have had to try it if Brian hadn't left her penniless. Yes, it was all his fault.

Instead of searching through her infernal Purse of a Million Pockets, she dumped everything out on the coffee table to find her phone. She called her husband, who answered, much to her surprise. Brian quickly came to regret that decision, because she proceeded to, as she had said she would, rip him a new one. There was much cursing and name calling, and that was all before he managed to say hello.

In summary, Griffin told Brian that he was despicable, untrustworthy, a flake, and a total idiot. She also threatened legal action for taking all their money, although she figured that was probably futile. But it was not futile to go after half his retirement assets, so she threatened that too. And she demanded custody of Clancy. Not negotiable.

Clancy was a rescue, and even though Griffin was not much of a dog person, Brian had insisted on adopting the thing. Within a week, Griffin was in love. Now she told Brian if he didn't hand over Clancy when she got home, she'd make sure he regretted it for the rest of his life. Brian agreed to give up Clancy, told her the new feisty Griffin was kind of hot, and then she hung up on him.

Feeling much better, she went to join her grandmothers.

The three of them now sat under a shade umbrella by the pool of the fancy resort spa hotel place, sipping San Pellegrinos. It was a day for taking it easy, and they were thinking about what to do next. Perhaps they would stay at the resort for a little while longer before going home. It was about three in the afternoon by this point, and as humid as all get-out.

"This weather is oppressive," said Delphine. "Southern California is so much nicer."

"Maybe it's because you're wearing a jacket," said Griffin.

"It's a blazer, not a jacket. But you're right." Delphine took her blazer off and hung it with care on the back of her chair. "Better, but still as humid as a sauna."

"I love it!" said Marge, who had on a sleeveless jumpsuit with a bird-of-paradise floral print. She moved her chair into the sun and lifted her chin to the sky, a huge grin on her face. "Sure beats the slammer!"

It seemed that the two grandmas had recovered well enough from the previous night's excitement, and Griffin was finally starting to recover from the events of her day too. She felt clear-headed and proud of herself for standing up to Brian. She felt better than she had in a long time.

"Wanna get some appetizers?" asked Marge.

"No thank you," said Delphine, yawning.

"I'm fine," said Griffin. She felt okay but had no appetite. She didn't have the stomach for crime, it seemed.

Marge shrugged. "There are no cute guys here," she said, pulling down her sunglasses to look at the people in the pool. "That was one nice thing about hanging out with the Blingsters. We attracted hunks like bees to honey."

"Yes, well, those days are behind you," said Delphine in a clipped voice.

Marge raised both hands in surrender. "Oh, don't I know it! I'm heading straight back to Oklahoma after all this." She looked toward the outdoor bar along one side of the pool. "Maybe." She got up from the table, straightened the front of her jumpsuit, and mussed her hair to perfection. "How do I look?"

When it became apparent Delphine wasn't going to answer, Griffin said, "Like a million bucks." Delphine glared at her granddaughter.

"Don't wait up," said Marge, and walked to the bar where she shimmied her way onto a barstool next to a white-haired gentleman wearing a Hawaiian shirt and fedora.

"She's incorrigible," said Delphine. Griffin had to agree.

"Hello there," said a voice from behind them. Which sounded a lot like Rolly's. Speaking of incorrigible.

"Hello, Detective Magnusson," said Delphine.

Without waiting to be asked to join them (which didn't bother Griffin, but she could tell Delphine was slightly affronted), Roland sat down next to Griffin and placed a tall glass of beer on the table. He wore sunglasses and his usual well-fitting T-shirt, but today he had on shorts. When she looked at his face it showed a hint of a smile, and she wondered if he'd caught her looking at his legs.

"Day off?" she asked him.

"Sort of," he said, with no further explanation.

Griffin looked over at Marge, still sitting at the bar. She was laughing hysterically, with one hand on her chest and the other on the shoulder of her gentleman friend. She was a real pro.

"How is everything back at the station?" Delphine asked Roland.

"Fine," he said, in a tone that implied things were anything but fine.

Delphine scrutinized him. "And by fine, you mean what, exactly?"

Roland sighed and leaned back in his chair. "She's free to

leave. She'll have to come back to appear in court as a witness against the other three, but for now she can go home."

"That's fair," said Delphine.

He looked at Griffin. "Please, in the name of all things holy, take her home," he said.

"I know you mean my grandma. But which one?"

"Both. Either. I don't care, just … Please."

Delphine laughed.

"I can't guarantee I can get anyone to go anywhere," said Griffin.

"Nor should you have to, Griffin," said Delphine. "We'll do our best to get Marge out of Florida, Detective Magnusson, I can't promise anything. As for myself, I don't plan on staying much longer."

He looked disappointed that he couldn't get more assurances from either of them. "I guess that'll have to do," he said. "Marge's car has been impounded, and you'll need to get her things out of that beach house."

"We'll do that tomorrow," Griffin said. "I don't think she had much in that place other than clothes." Griffin couldn't imagine that G-ma would have much need for so many evening dresses and fancy outfits in Enid, Oklahoma.

"Yeah, but she had a helluva lot of clothes," he pointed out.

"We'll take care of it," Delphine told him.

"The house was so trashed that the owners may sue the women for damages," said Roland.

Griffin laughed. "They might need to condemn that place."

He smiled. "Maybe. You should probably check whether her name is on the lease or not. That could be another headache for you."

"Thank you, we will," said Delphine.

Griffin watched as Roland's expression became dark again. Then he leaned forward in his chair so fast that Delphine jumped a little in her seat. He gave her a sharp look and seemed to puff up with irritation. "Let's just be clear. I don't like any of this one bit. I don't know what strings you pulled, lady, but this is my domain and I really hope I don't see you around here again."

Delphine gave him a saccharine smile. "Likewise, Rolly."

Griffin almost spit out her Pellegrino.

He seemed to be satisfied with her response, such as it was, and began to relax a little. Griffin watched them size each other up. She could learn a few things from both of them. Especially Delphine, who had refused to offer any details about how she'd managed to spring Marge from jail. It was better to play your hand close to the vest, and Griffin vowed to try to remember that.

"How long are you staying in Florida?" Roland asked them.

Delphine said, "I thought I'd treat Griffin and Marge to a few days here at the resort before we all leave. I'd like to try one of those hot stone massages, and maybe a yoga class." She glanced in Griffin's direction.

"Yes to the massage, hard pass on the yoga."

Roland looked at Griffin for a long moment, then said, "Well, just stay out of trouble."

"No guarantees," said Delphine, and when he turned to look at Griffin again, she gave him the most innocent smile she could muster.

CHAPTER 32

Marge settled on a stool right next to the man in the Hawaiian shirt. As she waited for the bartender to come over, she reflected on how much her life had changed in the last few months. She'd had some fun times over the years, and things had been exciting when her and Ziffy's love was fresh and new. Other than the birth of her sons, the Blingsters were the highlight so far. And those days appeared to be gone.

She tried to get a better look at the man next to her out of the corner of her eye. He'd caught her attention from across the patio, and up close he wasn't disappointing. Even though the Blingster era was over, maybe there was another fresh and new chapter waiting to begin.

"What can I get you?" the bartender asked as she placed a coaster on the bar in front of Marge.

"How 'bout a sea breeze?" asked Marge. The woman nodded and moved off to make her drink.

"Good choice," said the man sitting next to her.

Marge looked at him and feigned surprise, like she hadn't noticed him before now and he definitely wasn't the reason she'd come over to the bar. Her gaze drifted down to his drink. "It is?" she asked with more fake innocence.

"That's what I have," he said, holding up his glass.

"Well lookee there. That's a coincidence, isn't it!" she said.

"Like it was meant to be," he said with an inviting smile.

She smiled back. "Maybe so."

She took the opportunity of making small talk to get a better look at him from behind her sunglasses and went through her usual checklist. When he smiled at her, it appeared that his teeth were in good shape. The fedora made it hard to tell what his hair situation was, so that was still a question mark. Baldness wasn't a deal breaker, but at their age, men with their own hair were in huge demand. He seemed slender enough, not carrying too much of that dreaded weight around the middle, which meant less risk to his heart. All good ... Now for step two.

"Are you here on vacation with your wife?" she asked. The bartender brought her drink and set it down in front of her.

"No sirree, I'm here all by my lonesome," he said.

Marge picked up her drink. "I'll drink to that," she said.

He raised his glass and said, "Skål!"

They clinked their glasses. Marge removed the little paper umbrella from her cocktail, and they took sips of their drinks.

"My name is Willard," said the man. "Willard Kolbjörn." He removed his hat as a greeting, revealing a full head of salt-and-pepper hair.

Hooray! thought Marge.

"Nice to meet you, Willard, I'm Marge." She resisted the strong temptation to call him Willie. It was her natural inclination to do so, but it didn't seem like he'd appreciate it very much. "Kolbjörn, huh? Now why does that sound familiar?"

"Oh that's an easy one. You're thinking of the Kolbjörn line of furniture at Ikea, a very popular collection of indoor-outdoor cabinets and shelves." He beamed as he settled his hat back on his head.

Marge wasn't sure that Ikea furniture was what she'd been thinking of, but she also didn't know how else she would know such a strange name. She shrugged. "Okay. Are you Swedish?"

"I'm as Swedish as köttbullar!" he said. He put a finger to his nose. "That means meatballs."

"Oh! Haha!" She leaned forward and put a hand on Willard's shoulder as she let out a hearty guffaw. The man was so dorky it was downright adorable. She thought she might already be a little bit in love. But she had a few more tests to run.

"Where are you from, Marge?" asked Willard. "Are you here on your own?"

He showed interest in knowing more about her, which meant he passed that test with flying colors. Marge was cautiously starting to root for him. "Oh, me? I'm from Oklahoma. I came out here all by myself to go on a cruise, but I met some ladies who live near here, and we had so much fun that I decided to stay. But that's all over now. I'll be here a little while longer, then I'm supposed to leave to go back home."

"Oh, that's a shame," he said.

"Tell me about it. Anyway, how about you? Are you here on vacation?"

"Yes, that's right," he said. "It's nice to get away from the humdrum of everyday life, isn't it? You look like someone who would understand that." He winked at her.

Marge blushed. "Believe me, Willard, I get it!"

They chatted for a few more minutes, exchanging basic information—number of kids and grandkids, favorite TV shows, and the like. Within minutes Marge was completely smitten, and she was almost positive he was too. When he asked her out on a date for that night, she accepted without hesitation.

"Shitfire!" she said, when she realized that perhaps she was expected to spend time with Griffin and Delphine. Griffin was nice—a sweet girl, really—but Delphine seemed like a total square. The poor woman probably didn't have any friends or hobbies. Well too bad for her! Marge was a hot commodity here in Florida and she was going to make hay while the sun shone.

"Something wrong?" asked Willard.

"I don't know. I'm here with my granddaughter and her other

grandma. They might expect me to have dinner with them tonight."

"Oh," said Willard, who looked crestfallen.

"Don't worry," said Marge. "I'll just tell them tough potatoes, I have big plans tonight with my hot new friend!"

Willard perked up at that.

"But come with me and let me introduce you to them," said Marge. "They're right over—" She turned around to point at Griffin and Delphine's table and noticed Detective Hottie McHotterson was there too. "Well shitfire again," she said.

"What is it now?"

Marge stood up and pulled on the sleeve of Willard's Hawaiian shirt. "Nothing you need to worry about, sweetie," she said. "But when we get to the table, don't say too much and definitely don't make eye contact with the man who's sitting there. He's bad news." Hottie McHotterson might have been hot, but he was also a real stick in the mud.

"Okie dokie," said Willard, and they made their way over to the table where Griffin, Delphine, and the detective sat.

Marge swayed onto the balls of her toes and then back onto her heels as she spoke. "Everyone, meet Willard. Willard, meet everyone."

Willard removed his fedora again and bowed—actually bowed! If that didn't impress them all, she didn't know what would.

"Hello, everyone," Willard said, without taking his eyes off Marge, who blushed again.

"Hello," said Delphine, who appeared to be giving her new beau the eagle-eye.

Marge scowled. If Delphine tried to steal her man, the woman would have another thing coming. She tried to send Delphine a telepathic message: *Keep your mitts off him, he's mine.*

Griffin said, "Hi," and smiled, always the epitome of politeness.

Detective Hottie nodded but said nothing.

"Me and Willard are going out to dinner tonight," Marge said with a big smile. "He says he knows a place where they sell fresh clams by the gallon!"

Everyone at the table seemed perplexed by this but no one said anything. What was so hard to understand? Dinner with a man, that wasn't rocket science. Okay, clams by the gallon might be weird but whatever, she'd roll with it.

"Pick me up in the lobby at 5:00?" she asked Willard, giving his arm a squeeze.

"Make it 4:30," he said, winking at her before putting his hat back on and bowing to everyone again. He left the pool area and Marge sat down at the table.

"Pretty cute, huh?" she said. "And from what I can tell, those are his original teeth."

"A definite plus," said Delphine.

CHAPTER 33

"Welp, I'm off for a nap before my big date," said Marge. She gave everyone at the table a little wave and left the pool area.

Griffin looked at Rolly, who seemed perfectly at ease in the sunny, humid environment. He'd finished his beer and leaned back in his chair with his sunglasses now perched on top of his head. She wondered if he was as relaxed as he looked.

In a moment of weakness, or attraction (same thing, really), she considered telling him about the Moes. It might help with his investigation, and there was no reason why Delphine couldn't know about them too.

"There's something I should probably tell you," she said.

When Roland realized she was talking to him, he leaned forward.

"Maybe it'll help you with the Blingsters' case."

"The who?" he asked.

"That's what they called themselves," said Delphine. "Marge and her friends."

"Okay. Do you know what she's talking about?" Roland asked Delphine.

She gave a noncommittal shrug, and they both looked at Griffin.

"You know that diner, Little Moe's? Well, Little Moe and her husband Big Moe are the ones who were buying the jewelry from the Blingsters. They use the diner to conduct business, but also Big Moe is a podiatrist, and I wouldn't be surprised if they use that business too."

Roland pursed his lips as he thought. "Now that makes sense," he said.

"What?" asked Griffin.

"The podiatrist thing. I was wondering what the connection was. What else?"

"That's it. I mean, I don't have any hard evidence, but I overheard them talking and I've seen them with some pretty questionable people."

Delphine said, "I believe if you watch both locations, you'll come up with something. They've been in business for a while. The Blingsters weren't their only customers."

"Can we please not call them that?" said Roland. "It makes them sound like some kind of social club."

"But that's what they were, in a way," said Delphine. "Griffin, why are you giving me the evil eye?"

"You knew. All this time."

"Not the entire time, no."

"And here I thought I came up with something helpful," Griffin said, feeling deflated.

"You did," said Roland, in her defense. "This is great stuff."

"Don't forget, I've been in the business a long time," said Delphine.

"What business, exactly?" asked Roland, and again Delphine stayed silent.

"It wouldn't surprise me if you did a little digging and discovered the podiatrist office was also engaging in insurance fraud," said Griffin. "You might want to have your local feds look into it."

"Really?" asked Roland.

Delphine quirked an eyebrow. "Now that's something I hadn't thought about," she admitted.

Roland pulled his notepad out of the back pocket of his shorts. "Is that the kind of thing you did for the FBI in Dallas?"

"A little, yes," said Griffin. "I did a lot of securities fraud investigation, but it's kind of the same thing. You get good at looking for patterns while trailing the money."

Delphine nodded and smiled, and Griffin felt a little better.

"I'll have someone look into it, thanks," said Roland. He finished scribbling in his notepad and put it away.

They sat in silence for a while, then Delphine sighed. "I guess I should provide a little more information too," she said.

"This ought to be good," said Roland.

Griffin wondered what new bombshell Delphine would drop.

"Griffin, you got fired from the FBI is because of me."

"Excuse me now?" said Griffin, gripping the armrests of her chair. Of all the possible bombshells, that one had been farthest from her mind.

"Maybe I should leave," said Roland, looking like he'd rather be anywhere than at their table.

"No, please stay," Griffin told him. "I need a witness. Spill it, old lady."

Delphine shot her a disapproving look but continued. "You were staying there because it was safe. You were underutilized. Your boss was a jerk, and you were bored out of your mind."

"Seriously. How do you *know* all that?" asked Griffin.

"I thought we'd gone over this," said Delphine.

Nonetheless, Griffin was baffled.

Apparently, so was Roland. "You got your own granddaughter fired," he said.

"Yes, Roland," Delphine said, sounding like she was having to explain herself to a five-year-old.

"Gosh, thanks, Grandma," said Griffin.

"Of course that was before all the Brian stuff," said Delphine as she waved her hand. "The timing isn't great, I admit."

Griffin opened her mouth to speak but nothing came out.

"He wasn't good enough for you, dear," said Delphine.

"I agree," said Roland, and both women looked at him. "He sounds like a real ass hat."

"Oh, he is," said Delphine.

Griffin still couldn't believe her grandmother's confession. "So now what? I have no job, no home, no money, no husband. All I have is Clancy."

Roland frowned. "Who's Clancy?"

"My dog," said Griffin. "He's a Whoodle."

"Isn't that a word game?"

"What? No! He's part poodle and part Wheaton Terrier."

"Sure," said Roland, unimpressed.

Griffin glared at Delphine and said, "Clancy is the only other creature on the planet who loves me."

"Please," said Delphine. "I'm not falling for that. But since I am partially responsible for getting you into this mess, I promise I'll help you get out of it."

"Partially?" said Griffin.

"Brian would have left you at some point."

Griffin thought for a moment. "You can start making it up to me with a fresh seafood dinner."

"Deal," said Delphine. "Rolly, would you care to join us?"

Griffin tensed, and Roland seemed to also.

"Oh, well, I'd love to, but I need to be home for dinner tonight," he said, and he rose from the table. "In fact, I should be leaving now."

Griffin's heart sank a tiny bit but she reminded herself that he was married, and if she didn't watch it, she'd be in danger of doing something just as stupid as Shelby Wafer had, and there was no way she wanted to be like Shelby Wafer.

Delphine and Griffin stood too.

"May we never meet again," Roland said as he shook Delphine's hand. She smiled.

"May we … I don't know what," he said to Griffin as he shook her hand.

"Same," she said.

She watched him walk away and felt very confused.

CHAPTER 34

Griffin and Delphine enjoyed a delicious seafood dinner as planned, and the three ladies spent the following morning picking up the rest of Marge's things from the beach house and bringing them to the resort. It seemed to take forever, and by the time they were done, their suite looked more like a clothing boutique than a hotel room. Griffin tried to convince Marge that she wouldn't need all those outfits and accessories back home, but G-ma wouldn't hear of it. Every last jumpsuit was coming with her, she insisted.

The beach house had been an absolute mess, even worse than before, and the carport looked empty without G-ma's car parked there. Otto was gone, and Marge was understandably sad, but Griffin tried to explain it was for the best. Better to have loved and lost, and all that jazz. Unfortunately her pep talk didn't do much to console Marge, and she had a hard time believing her own words as well. The car had been a work of art.

Griffin was still a little mad at Delphine, despite the conciliatory dinner. Whenever she remembered her grandmother's confession, she got mad all over again, and at times the morning had gotten quite frosty. Around midday,

Delphine pulled Griffin aside and convinced her it would be okay, and that she would help Griffin out, and the ice started to melt.

After a delicious lunch in the resort's restaurant, they all got hot-stone massages and went swimming. It was a lovely afternoon and Griffin enjoyed hanging out with both of her unusual grandmas at the same time. It hadn't happened often in her life, so it was a nice treat.

Sharing the hotel room with her two grandmothers wasn't too bad either. The roll-away bed was quite comfortable, and all of them seemed to get along well enough in close quarters. Although G-ma hogged the bathroom while getting ready for her dates with Willard.

When Marge returned from her second date night with Willard at around 8:00, they started packing up all her clothes.

That morning, they'd decided that they would all fly home the next evening. They had gone to the local UPS store and picked up some boxes to pack Marge's clothes in, and tomorrow they would take the boxes back to UPS and send them out. Then, if there was time, Delphine said she would treat them to one last massage, or maybe a facial.

Griffin didn't want to know how much it would cost Marge to send so many boxes, and she also didn't want to know what funds her G-ma was going to use to pay for it all. As far as she knew, the police hadn't checked her finances. Either Delphine had done a thorough job of getting Marge out of trouble, or Detective Magnusson was a terrible detective. She'd bet on the former. But no one ever told her anything, so she had no idea what the real story was. Just like so many things when it came to her family.

Marge went into the bathroom to change out of her date jumpsuit and into her jammies, as Griffin and Delphine began sorting out all the clothes.

"This is insane," said Delphine, holding up a purple-sequined handbag.

"The bag or the amount of stuff?" asked Griffin.

"Both."

Marge came back out of the bathroom and sat on the edge of her bed, piled high with more clothes.

"Me and Willard are getting married!" she said.

Griffin dropped the pair of shoes she'd been holding. "Excuse me?"

"Yeah, in a couple of months. We got engaged tonight!"

"Congratulations?" said Delphine, who then looked at Griffin with a shocked expression.

"Yeah, congratulations, G-ma," said Griffin, who shrugged at Delphine.

"Thanks!" Marge said, then held out her left hand so that everyone could see the shiny engagement ring. It was beautiful.

"Nice," said Griffin. "How did Willard get you a ring so quickly?"

"This old thing? It's just something I had lying around," said Marge. "Ain't she a beaut? Now I have a real excuse to wear it!"

Delphine covered her face with her hands and Griffin knew exactly what the woman was thinking, because she was thinking the same thing. What had they done by springing G-ma? Griffin had put Delphine into a no-win situation by helping Marge. She crossed her fingers that none of them would come to regret their actions any more than they already did.

"Anyhow," continued Marge, "I'm moving into his townhouse tomorrow." She looked around the room at the piles of stuff. "So we can pack all this up and take it right over there! Willard will help, of course."

"Of course," said Delphine.

"Where does he live?" asked Griffin.

"Not far from here. In fact, he lives real close to the Blingsters' beach house. Isn't that something?"

"Yes it is," said Delphine.

Griffin pondered this. Up until now, she had thought Willard was a visitor to Florida, like the three of them were. Or at most, he was here on a trip from another part of the state. She'd assumed he and G-ma would have a couple of fun dates before everyone went their separate ways, back to their regular lives. It had never occurred to Griffin that he was local. What was he doing staying in a resort so close to home?

She looked at Delphine for guidance, and her grandmother nodded her head in a way that said she'd handle this. Of course she would.

"Detective Magnusson told us that the Blingsters are no more. They're all still in jail, likely for some time."

G-ma dropped her arms to her sides and tilted her head at Delphine for dramatic effect. "They could be living right next door to Willard and me for all I care. I'll never be tempted to do anything illegal ever again. You won't even catch me getting a parking ticket!"

Delphine's reminder about the Blingsters' demise and G-ma's declaration of going cold turkey from a life of crime made Griffin feel somewhat better, but they still knew nothing about darling Willard. Vern, Smitty, and Big El had looked harmless enough too, until you got up close. Willard could be a smuggler, or a sociopath, or a politician.

Delphine placed a neatly folded stack of jumpsuits into a box. "Your Oklahoma family will miss having you around, Marge."

G-ma sighed. "And I'll miss them too. But this is true love, ladies. I'm running out of time to have some fun, you know?"

"I do know," said Delphine with a touch of wistfulness in her voice.

Griffin knew what she meant too. The end of her marriage made her realize that nothing was permanent. In some cases, that was a very good thing, however.

She still had so many questions, but if Delphine seemed to be okay with Marge's plan, she must have had her reasons and Griffin just didn't know what they were. Like maybe she'd already done a background check on Willard. In fact, Griffin would bet money that she had. They continued to pack in silence.

The last few days had helped Griffin forget about her troubles for a while. Her grandmas were picking up the tab for the resort, which she appreciated. She still hadn't told G-ma about Brian, and Delphine hadn't breathed a word, as far as she could tell. But she was going to have to face reality soon.

Every day she'd double-checked her bank accounts, but each login produced the same results: zero balance. And now the credit card bill was overdue. She'd told Brian off, which felt great, but her situation still seemed dire. As she placed a matching purse and shoe set into a box, she knew what she had to do. She needed to try to take the diamond to Big Moe again and wade back into that murky grey area.

This time it would be much riskier since she had told Roland about the Moes. Maybe he had already put them out of business. It was also possible that he might decide to bust Little Moe at the diner right when she happened to be there too. But desperation sometimes made people do foolish things, and she knew she was going to try again.

She certainly didn't want to be caught going through airport security with the giant gem, and even if she got it back to Fort Worth, she had doubts that she'd be able to figure out how to sell it there for a decent price. At least here in Florida she knew some questionable people. How exciting was that! She knew questionable people!

Griffin would take her chances with the Moes, and there was no sense in putting it off. It was early enough that she could say she was going out to get something from the drugstore and drive to the diner instead. She could always change her mind on the way there.

That beautiful diamond. Something about it was mesmerizing, transfixing. Maybe it was because it was so huge and beautiful, or maybe it held mystical properties. She ached to hold it again.

Just as she was wondering how she would get it out of the safe without drawing attention to herself, she noticed that Delphine and G-ma were arguing.

"But surely you can let me have one purse," Delphine said.

"Yeah, you can have one, but not that one! That's my special purse," said Marge. "Pick another one."

"Can't you just pick another special purse?"

"No."

"But this is the only one that's not ugly," snapped Delphine.

Here was Griffin's chance. She put down an armful of silk blouses and walked to the suite's closet as if she didn't have a care in the world. The closet was off a short hallway that led to the bathroom and the front door, out of view of her grandmas who were still arguing about purses. She stepped into the closet and typed the combination into the keypad. "Be cool, be cool," she whispered under her breath.

When the safe popped open, she took out her sport socks and clutched them in her fist.

"That's a strange thing to keep in a safe," Delphine said from right behind her.

Griffin panicked. What would be a good cover story for having put socks in a safe? But something else was far more panic-worthy. The socks felt way too light. About one large diamond too light.

"You're right. That was kind of stupid," Griffin said.

"What was stupid?" asked G-ma, joining them in the closet. She peered into the empty safe.

"Griffin put a pair of socks in the safe," said Delphine.

Griffin held up her clenched fist and gave her grandmas a weak smile.

"Oh yeah? Didja put something in the socks?" G-ma asked. "Wait, let me guess! Your cocaine stash!"

"Haha," was all Griffin could manage. All the blood rushed to her feet, leaving her light-headed.

Delphine gave Griffin a long look. "Jewelry, perhaps?"

"Oh, of course, that would make a lot more sense. Show us what you've got there, Griffy!" G-ma clapped her hands.

Griffin took a deep breath. "Okay."

Delphine held out her hand, and Griffin dumped the socks

into her grandmother's palm. They sprung open, bounced out of her hand, and landed on the floor with a little *floof* sound.

G-ma picked them up and turned each one inside out. "There's nothing in these!"

"That's right," Griffin said. "I put them in there for no reason. For a joke. Ha."

Where on earth had the diamond gone? The rumors must have been true—hotel staff really stole things from the safes in guests' rooms. She looked at her bouncy G-ma and the ever-observant Delphine. They weren't laughing.

"I'd say that one fell flat," said Marge.

"Yeah, I guess so," said Griffin.

G-ma wandered away and Delphine lingered, giving her one last reproachful look before returning to the bedroom to pack another box.

Griffin closed the safe, picked up her socks, and stood in the closet. She was screwed.

She couldn't tell her grandmothers about the diamond. She couldn't tell the hotel management that someone on their staff had stolen from her, either. Because then she might have to explain what she was doing with a giant diamond, or worse, be required to show proof it was hers. She couldn't do a single thing except try not to look too disappointed and go back to packing.

Even though she knew she shouldn't, she felt sad that her unusual find had disappeared. She still couldn't pinpoint exactly why she had taken it. But every time she'd gotten to hold it, it had given her a little thrill. Like she had a secret that might have been a little dangerous (or a lot), but also exciting and strangely compelling. Now that it was gone, she knew she wouldn't have been able to sell it after all. It had been too special.

Maybe she needed to get out more. Maybe there was some legitimate excitement she could add to her life. Because she didn't seem to be cut out for crime.

CHAPTER 35

The next morning, they had breakfast with Willard and then transported Marge's belongings to his beach house. It took four trips with both cars. His place was much nicer than the Blingsters' party house. Griffin felt relieved that her G-ma would be living in a comfortable space. However they still knew next to nothing about her new roomie.

By noon they were all starving and decided to grab lunch together. G-ma had suggested they go to Little Moe's Diner, but both Delphine and Griffin nixed that idea. They opted for a small taco place, not far from the resort. It was right on the water, and the view was lovely. It was a nice way to say goodbye (and good riddance) to Griffin's Florida trip.

They sat down at a picnic table to wait for their food. G-ma and Willard canoodled at one end, and Griffin and Delphine tried very hard not to look at them from the other end.

"You have a visitor," Delphine said to Griffin, and pointed to the parking lot. There was Roland's crappy unmarked police car.

"How did he know we were here?" asked Griffin.

"He tailed us from the resort, didn't you notice?" said Delphine.

"I am so terrible at all this." Griffin got up from the bench. "Excuse me for a moment."

She opened the passenger side door and slid into the front of the car next to Roland. "Don't you have anything better to do than watch us eat?" she asked him.

"I happen to have a vested interest in the three of you leaving the state of Florida," he said, and angled himself along the seat so he almost faced her.

"Well, I have some bad news for you then."

He looked crestfallen. "Oh no."

"Oh yes. Marge Flanders is staying in the area." Griffin was pleased she'd gotten to break the news.

Roland closed his eyes and muttered a string of curses under his breath.

"But don't worry," said Griffin. "She's promising to stay out of trouble now."

"I believe that about as much as I believe in the tooth fairy."

"That's your problem. I still believe in the tooth fairy," Griffin said, and when he looked at her, she smiled, and he did too.

"Did you catch the Moes?" she asked.

"Not yet, but they're being watched. If what you said is true, it shouldn't be long before they're out of business."

Griffin nodded. "Too bad—you won't be able to go back for another kelp smoothie."

"I'll find a way to manage."

They sat for a few beats in silence. "Your food is probably getting cold," he said.

"Do you want to come eat with us?" she asked, hoping he would say yes.

"I don't think that would be a good idea. But thank you."

She nodded. Yes, it probably wasn't a good idea.

"We're leaving tonight," she said.

"I know."

"How closely are you watching us?"

Roland gave her a look that questioned her intelligence. "Can you blame me?"

"No, I guess not."

They sat in silence some more. It felt as if neither of them wanted to end the conversation, but the things that they wanted to say next could not be said. So there was nothing to say.

"Maybe I'll see you around," she said, and put her hand on the door handle.

"That would be nice," said Roland. "I hope things work out for you at home."

"They will, one way or another. I hope the same for you," said Griffin, not being entirely truthful. When she was out of the car, she took a deep breath, poked her head back in, and said, "Call me sometime."

She closed the door and walked away before he had a chance to say anything else.

After lunch, Griffin and her grandmas checked out of the resort. Delphine and Griffin put their bags in the tiny rental car to go to the airport, and then helped G-ma put the last of her things in Willard's Buick.

Delphine said goodbye to the happy couple and walked to the rental car to wait for Griffin, giving her time for a proper farewell.

"I guess this is it, for a little while anyway," said Griffin. G-ma and Willard stood side-by-side as Griffin shook Willard's hand. "Take good care of her," she said, grinning. "Because if you don't, I'll come back and kick your ass."

Willard's eyes went wide with surprise, but he recovered nicely. "Oh, you betcha, Griffin, I'll take real good care of this little spitfire here." He reached an arm behind Marge's back and did something to her that made her jump with surprise. She let out a loud laugh and Griffin was thankful she hadn't seen whatever he'd done.

"I called your father earlier this morning to give him the good news," said G-ma, giving Griffin a hug.

"I know. I've gotten thirty texts from him in the last hour."

Griffin gave her grandma a big hug back. "Be careful, okay, G-ma? No more jewelry thieving … or thieving of any kind."

Marge nodded solemnly. "Of course not. I'm on the straight and narrow."

"Are you?" Griffin asked.

"Well, sure I am!" she exclaimed, putting one hand on her heart. "I left you your socks, didn't I?"

NEXT IN THE SERIES

The Big Cheese

Ballroom Dancing. Bandits. Bad Brie?

All Delphine Lougheed wants to do is enjoy a quiet retirement from her super-spy career. But someone is about to kick up a stink…

The Big Cheese is the second book in the Old School Mysteries series. Pick up your copy at your favorite retailer!

BOOKS BY ANDREA C. NEIL

OLD SCHOOL MYSTERIES

The Blingsters

The Big Cheese

Gone Grandpa

The Last Resort

THE BEVERLEY GREEN ADVENTURES

Beverley Green's First Adventure

Beverley Green's First Territorial Christmas

Beverley Green Finds True North

Beverley Green Comes Home

The Guthrie Short Stories

MICRO FICTION

Days Are Beautiful: 100 flash fiction stories

No Surprises: 100 flash fiction stories

Visit acneil.com for more information

ACKNOWLEDGMENTS

Just a quick thank you to everyone who has helped me on this journey. The last few years have been rough, but thanks to you this book is now out in the world and life is pretty good.

Thanks to my business partner and number one editor, Michele Chiappetta, for her steadfastness and excellent advice. And to Lauren Smith for her pro tips, and Meghan Jones for the editing help.

Another huge thanks to my good friend and amazing artist, Karen Lucrece Bates, for her artwork, patience, and friendship. Also her cats are super cute.

Thank you to my Beta Readers: Mary Ames, Alan Bates, and Deepti Zaremba, whose keen insight helped this book become better!

And to everyone else who's helped me get through it all … thank you!

Marcus Winkler

Deepti & Jan Zaremba

Lisa & Bill Neil

Dayl Workman

Julie Umansky

Lisa Bracken

Ellie Coppola

ABOUT THE AUTHOR

Andrea lives in Oklahoma but grew up in Southern California—and the latter will always be home in her heart. In 2015 she left a job in finance to follow her passion for writing and creating art. With age comes wisdom, or at least a few more stories to tell, and in 2018, Andrea began self-publishing quirky novels with the intention of brightening her readers' day. When she's not trying to get her own words onto a page, Andrea edits other people's writing, eats dark chocolate, and goes on walks if the weather's nice.

acneil.com

amazon.com/author/andreaneil
bookbub.com/profile/andrea-c-neil
facebook.com/andreacneil
instagram.com/andreacneil

www.ingramcontent.com/pod-product-compliance
Lightning Source LLC
Chambersburg PA
CBHW020038310726
48970CB00007B/2310